Returned

The Romani Realms Series

Book Three

by Mia Fox

Returned, Book 3, Romani Realms Series by Mia Fox
Published by Evatopia Press
http://www.evatopia.com
8447 Wilshire Blvd., Ste. 401, Beverly Hills, CA 90211
a division of Evatopia, Inc.

ISBN: 978-1-63099-053-4

Cover design by Eden Crane Design
http://www.edencranedesign.com/

Interior book design by Bob Houston eBook Formatting
www.facebook.com/eBookFormatting/info

See other titles by Mia Fox at www.miafox.net.

Stay in touch with Mia Fox

Twitter @MiaFoxBooks
Facebook www.facebook.com/MiaFoxBooks

Acknowledgements

Two years ago, when I wrote "Released," the first book in this series, I was just starting out in my indie writing journey. I didn't know many other authors and I hadn't yet developed a readership. I never expected to meet so many supportive people – a wonderful online world of writers and readers who love books as much as I do.

If you are holding this book, I sincerely thank you. Thank you as well to my Facebook fan base and the authors who support me on Twitter. You mean the world to me. I've been known to write stories "on demand" and if you need a smile, I welcome the challenge.

And in the times when I haven't risen to challenges, I've been fortunate to rely on the kindness of others. Sue Ann Brooks, you were a beacon of sunshine before this book was published. I thank you so much for your proofreading and critique. I hope this story met your expectations. Jessica Molina Ramirez, thank you for your continued friendship and support. I would be lost without you.

My beloved family...thank you for allowing me to pursue this crazy dream. I love you all.

Happiness can exist only in acceptance.

George Orwell

Prologue

T he black birds swarmed overhead, so many that the sky darkened. Below them, a wolf chased a girl through the woods, its pace just barely lagging her as if toying with its future prey. It nearly made her believe that she would escape by letting her gain a few feet, only to close the gap again.

Finally, when she stumbled over brambles and tree roots, causing her to fall, the wolf pounced as the black birds overhead knew it would. They let it feed to its satisfaction, and when it retreated, still having left plenty of meat on the bones, the birds descended upon the carrion.

Watching with disgust was Raven.

"They act like such animals," she said shaking her head.

Daniel looked at her with mild amusement. "A few months ago you would have gladly joined them."

She smiled at him, lowering her lashes coquettishly, "Well, I've turned over a new leaf...thanks to you. Doesn't watching this bother you?"

He placed his arm around her waist and led her up the path to his secluded home, hidden deep within the Romani Realms. "It's the Romani Realms. You can't let this place get under your skin or it will take your soul. Come on," he encouraged, leading the way. "Dinner is heating on the stove and it should be ready by now."

# # #

Chapter One

Samantha stared out the cafe window. Charlotte had insisted they try this place as it was written up in every magazine imaginable from those appealing to foodies to people watchers. The place was known for serving "farm to table" cuisine, which to Samantha loosely translated into a plate of vegetables with a meager scrap of chicken on top, all more expensive than any salad she had eaten before. She picked at her food while watching the pedestrians of Robertson Boulevard.

The Beverly Hills street was known to house many restaurants run by celebrity chefs where patrons jockeyed to get a table close to the sidewalk so their photo could be snapped by the paparazzi and they could later pretend it was such a nuisance. The area also heaved with chic boutiques, the kind that boasted the latest styles by aspiring designers who all seemed to go by only one name.

Normally, a stroll along this street on a sunny day would brighten Samantha's mood, but now she was happy for the opportunity to sit in one place and sip her tea quietly. Today's outing felt tiring as she followed Charlotte in her quest to find a wedding dress. She had promised Samantha they would also look for bridesmaid dresses, but the declaration was hardly a consolation prize.

"You're having fun, right?" Charlotte inquired, both hopeful and overly cheery.

"Sure I am."

"That sounds convincing."

"Charlotte, I'm sorry. I'm trying. Really, I am."

"But?" her friend prodded.

"Do you know why I have the personality of a troubled goth girl? I just feel all dark and sad inside."

Charlotte pulled her friend into a hug, gently rubbing her palm against her back in small circles. She had done the same when Samantha would often find her way to Charlotte's house after realizing her mother wasn't coming home again. Work had been a priority. Then a new man was more important. Soon after, Samantha was alone. It was the same way she felt today.

"You know what sounds like fun?" Charlotte asked rhetorically, still trying to cheer her friend. "Lunch on Montana Avenue. The Courtyard Kitchen beckons us."

Samantha stabbed a leaf of wilted lettuce, held it up, and inquired, "Isn't this lunch?"

"Technically this is brunch. We could eat our way through the day. It beats going home and watching you mope around there," Charlotte offered.

"You ready?" Samantha didn't address Charlotte's observation of her behavior. She just wanted to do exactly what Charlotte already suspected – sit at home and wallow in her own sadness. She dropped a few bills on the check tray and then tossed her napkin onto the table, heading for the door. Charlotte followed, struggling to catch up to her friend's fast pace out the door.

Finally, Samantha stopped in front of a shop, but her gaze didn't lie on the clothes displayed in the window. She looked at a guy who resembled Daniel, tall and strong with brown hair and green eyes, smiling admiringly at his girl who twirled in front of him, modeling a new dress.

"He looks just like Daniel," Samantha noted. "For a moment, I thought..."

Charlotte reached out and touched her shoulder. "Maybe Banana Pancakes will help?

We could sit outside. It's like eating and shopping all at once only the merchandise are the gorgeous guys that will be walking along just for our sheer enjoyment. What do you say?"

Samantha shook her head with a glum expression. "Not interested. I don't care about any guy other than Daniel."

Charlotte nodded, knowing that you can't just turn off your heart. If it were that easy, she probably would have walked away from Phineas when she learned he was a demon gypsy who had once been aligned with Raven, the girl who had originally sent Samantha into the Romani Realms and caused such upheaval in their lives.

"I wonder if he thinks about me as much as I do him?" Samantha asked with a little shrug of her shoulders.

"Of course he thinks of you," Charlotte chided. "It was obvious that he cared deeply about you. But...you have to go on, Samantha. I know it's not the same as a break up, but people separate for all sorts of reasons. Some move away. Some...I don't know...I just know that it isn't healthy to pine over someone that you can never have again."

Samantha bit her lip, forcing a smile in order not to cry. Whenever she felt this way, she would relish the memory of being with him. He was, after all, the first man she had ever loved.

"It's harder than you know. I was in the Romani Realms for three months before you all arrived to save me. It sounds like a short time, but it was long enough to fall hard for him. Time doesn't pass the way it does here. It was..." she shook her head, struggling to find the right word.

"I can't imagine how hard it was for you," Charlotte offered.

"Each day in that purgatory is three times the length of one here. I've been back for six months. You might think that's just a blip in time and for here, that may be true. But over there..." her voice trailed off. "Over there, it's a year-and-a-half. Enough time to forget. It makes me so sad to think that he's...moved on."

Charlotte raised her eyebrows and winced, not wanting to state what was on her mind, but Samantha knew. They had been friends long enough to know how to finish each other's sentences and to know what the other was feeling. "Don't say it," Samantha noted.

"I didn't say anything," Charlotte jumped. "It's just..."

"I know. I think about him being there and how lonely it must be. I don't know what I want for him.

Part of me wants to do the right thing and hope that he's moved on because I love him. But, because I love him...I want him to love me back. To still think of me."

Charlotte nodded her head in understanding. "Sam? I know this isn't what you want to hear, and I'm sorry, but I just can't keep it to myself. Please know that I'm saying this because I care about you."

"What is it?"

"I don't just want you to occupy your time. It's not about going to lunch or getting a new hobby. I think you should forget Daniel." The moment the words left her mouth, the leaves of the trees rustled up and down, back and forth, as if nodding in agreement. She looked up and felt a sudden chill in the air that only intensified when she looked at the determined green eyes of her friend.

"I've tried. But as they say, you never forget your first love."

"You can't go back there and he can't ever leave," Charlotte reminded.

"I know."

The two friends walked arm in arm, continuing to window shop, and for a brief moment Charlotte felt relief. She had said her peace and her friend seemed to take her advice. But like so many precious gifts in life, the moment was fleeting as Samantha said the words Charlotte dreaded to hear.

"But, you managed to find me...and bring me back."

"Samantha, no. You can't think that way."

A wry smile played across Samantha's features, a look that was all at once sad and hopeful. "It's the only thought that has kept me going. It wakes me in the morning and sees me to bed at night. And as I look into that night sky, I have to wonder if Daniel isn't doing the same. Maybe...just maybe...we'll find our way back to each other."

# # #

Chapter Two

R aven took care in setting the table, a large rectangular piece that based from the circles engrained in its oak looked as if it had been around for centuries and could have told stories of the families who sat around it before. After arranging two place settings, she brought over a vase with bright, pink azaleas that were a welcome contrast to the dark skies outside.

"That's nice," Daniel noted as he walked over from the adjoining kitchen. He looked at home in the kitchen wearing oven mitt gloves and carrying a heavy, porcelain stew pot in a happy shade of robin egg blue. It brimmed with the smell of a home-cooked meal. Whipping the cover off with a flourish, he raised his eyebrows at Raven. "Looks good enough to eat, huh?"

She laughed at his exuberance. "You are an amazing cook," she agreed.

"I prefer the term – chef," he emphasized with mock hurt, proceeding to spoon out the thick broth that was embellished with tasty vegetables from his own garden into two bowls. After setting the pot back on the stove to stay warm, he came back to his seat and didn't waste any time in digging into the meal, stopping only to pat the seat next to him.

Raven acknowledged the hint and took her regular seat, a place she had already set right next to Daniel. While he devoured another mouthful of his masterpiece, he looked up noticing that Raven hadn't touched hers yet.

"Aren't you hungry? I made a trade with one of the soulless ones for some chicken. Vegetables for three meals in exchange for enough meat for this stew. Not my best deal, I have to admit, but you're worth it," he winked at her, chuckling at his own joke.

Raven picked up her spoon and tucked into the stew. "It's delicious. I'm a nightmare in the kitchen. When I was younger, Suki tried to show me how to cook. She was always whipping up some Southern delicacy, but my attempts would end up down the sink."

"Do you miss her?"

A choked and small chuckle escaped Raven's mouth, but she immediately quieted it. "That's a complicated question. There's no point in thinking about the past." The moment the words left her, Raven covered her mouth as if realizing her faux pas. "Shoot, I didn't mean that. I'm sorry."

"It's okay," he said, knowing that she referred to his troubled past as well. Daniel had spent years...decades...in the Romani Realms but was still plagued by occasional nightmares of his life before. The details were murky with the exception of his rescuing a small girl and then waking when he could no longer see her.

"You're right. I always lived in the moment before I met you...or anyone else," he said, a subtle reference to Samantha. With her wild mane of red hair and a disposition that was equally charged, he couldn't help falling in love with her. That was, before she returned to the world of the present three months earlier...a virtual life sentence for one alone in the Romani Realms. It was hard for him to believe that he had now spent double that time with Raven.

The silence enveloped them once more, but it was neither awkward nor uncomfortable. It was a quiet existence that both of them had grown to appreciate. The only sound was Raven's spoon that stirred the bottom of her bowl. But Daniel, always attentive to her, noticed that she paid more attention to moving the stew in circles rather than lift any to her mouth.

"Do you want some bread to go with it?" He motioned to her bowl, which still remained nearly full.

Raven jumped to attention at his suggestion. "I can get it."

But Daniel no sooner grabbed her arm. "Sit. Relax. Come on, Raven," he said, still holding her hand and encouraging her to sit close to him once more. "Just be."

His relaxing tone calmed her and she recovered from the urge to run away, even if it were only to the next room. "I just meant that it's delicious without, but if you want some, I can slice it. You keep eating."

"How come you're not more interested in food tonight? You seem so quiet. You're downright docile."

Raven smiled in spite of her obvious melancholy mood. "Not the Raven you once knew?"

Placing his spoon down, Daniel turned to face her. "You've heard the talk, haven't you?"

Her head bobbed, but otherwise she didn't verbalize an answer. It was too difficult.

"I've heard it too." Daniel's tone, although hesitant, caused Raven to place her elbows on the table, her head in her hands.

"More about an uprising?" she asked in a small voice that seemed so out of character for her.

Nodding, Daniel turned Raven's chair so that her body faced him. Opening his legs, he pulled her chair in between them and held her hands. "You're safe here," he said and reached his arms around her waist as she dropped her head forward so it came to rest on his chest.

"But for how long?" In spite of how nice it felt to be that close to Daniel, his woodsy cologne reaching her nostrils, the sight of his broad chest prominently before her, Raven forced herself to keep a distance. She got up and paced to the other side of the small, but quaint family room. A cheery, yellow towel was draped over the freshly baked bread that had been a point of discussion earlier. It was cooling on the bar that divided the family room from the kitchen, its scent filling the entire home with comfort...a comfort that was rapidly vanishing.

Raven turned, sensing Daniel had come near her as he often did when she was out of arm's reach. He reached for something behind her and in that moment she both wished for his arms to envelop her waist and prayed they wouldn't. As if sensing her hesitancy, he merely pinched off a corner of the loaf.

"Your silence is answer enough." Still when he didn't respond, she repeated her question. "How long, Daniel?"

"I don't know, Raven. They seem...restless."

She nodded, knowing exactly what he was implying. She had been that way herself, back when Samantha and Charlotte has accidentally gotten themselves trapped in the Romani Realms. The only way to appease the trapped souls who lived in this in-between world was to feed them with an innocent, allowing them to take over a pure soul.

Raven never believed that Charlotte would avenge Samantha's death, but then again, she never would have expected her own lover, Phineas, to end up with the girl the prophecy of the Realm named the White Dove, one-third of a Triad that would have ultimate power to shape and manipulate time.

Yes, she had underestimated both Charlotte and Samantha, not to mention Suki, who had been released by both of them. The three of them had been like a burrowed tick under her skin, incessantly noticeable no matter how much you wanted to ignore them. Some people just don't know when to stay put, she thought to herself.

Like that blood-sucking parasite, they just took and took everything she once had. Suki had taken James without even knowing that he had once belonged to her. And then, after centuries of grooming Phineas into a proper demon gypsy, along comes Charlotte with her big blue eyes, silky blonde hair and an innocence that permeates her translucent skin. She made him fall in love with her. Just. Like. That.

What did they expect? Taking Samantha's life was par for the course. It's not like anyone would have really missed that wild red head. No parents, no boyfriend, and truly only Charlotte to care for her. Her life was necessary collateral damage. Without an innocent, the soulless ones would have come for Raven. She reflected on how different she was then to now.

Now, her choices would have been different. When she was in power the only way to stay there was to show her strength. She had to make the soulless ones believe that she reigned the Romani Realms and the council did as she saw fit. She had enough power to keep them from bothering her. It was a case of survival of the fittest. But that was before Charlotte did the unthinkable and willingly entered the Romani Realms to offer her life for that of Samantha's.

They would have accepted it too, and Raven could have gone on living quite happily, thank you very much. But Suki interfered. Raven sat still thinking about how once Suki would have sacrificed everything for her...not her Releasors. Maybe it was that jealousy that started everything. She had to ask herself: Was she hurt that Phineas chose Charlotte or that Suki did?

"What are you thinking about?" Daniel brought her back to the present and his cozy home.

"Choices," she answered simply. "The right ones and the wrong ones I've made."

"Hopefully, I fall under the first?"

"You do," she smiled, and touched his cheek.

If only she had met Daniel first, then none of this might have happened. As their genie, Suki had to follow Samantha and then Charlotte into the Realms. It became god-damn Grand Central Station, with James, her Shade, jumping through time along with Phineas too. They might as well have hosted a darned dinner party – oh right, they did. Even Samantha faired well having met Daniel. Three happy couples gathered round the table...this very table.

Raven wiped a tear at the memory. A memory that didn't include her.

"What's wrong? I don't want you to worry," Daniel reassured her, believing Raven was only contemplating the possibility of an uprising. She had good reason to worry. The soulless ones wanted more than innocents to feed on; they wanted revenge. Most of them viewed Raven with intense hatred when it was discovered that she allowed not one, but two innocents to leave their land.

The knowledge spread and she was brought before the high council, the very one that she used to rule. Talk of the Triad was brought up, but Raven was careful to dismiss it. After all, it couldn't be proved. Only Suki knew for certain if her own powers could align with two others and she was most careful of whom she shared that knowledge.

There was a time when Raven had hoped that she and Phineas would control the Triad with a third, to be determined. It seemed like a lifetime ago. Time. Anyone who could manipulate time in this place would gain absolute power. They could make time pass quickly or wreak havoc by doing the brutal opposite. Time was the only thing that nobody could control.

Daniel nudged her and she offered a weak smile at his attempt to lighten the mood. It was hard not to smile when looking at Daniel with his wavy, brown hair that always looked as if he had just jumped out of bed. And in spite of the fact that sleep didn't come easy in the Realms, his eyes always twinkled with a sunny disposition mirrored by adorable dimples. Not to mention, he had a body that was hard and strong from working the land. He was truly a good person, down to the depth of his core. Looking at him filled her with hope that she could remain with him always and the happiness would continue. They had both worked hard to bury their memories, or at least put them to rest. They had each suffered loss and weaker people may not have been able to recover, but the Romani Realms had a strange way of bringing people together. Particularly if one considered the slim choices among those who still had their souls intact.

Raven turned and rested her head against Daniel's shoulder and sighed with relief. In this moment, no matter how fleeting, she had found a slice of happiness.

# # #

Chapter Three

C harlotte bounded through the door of the Malibu home calling Phineas' name. It was a gorgeous day, the type that begged for pictures and posts. A gentle ocean breeze drifted through the window and the sun made the water glisten like a million diamonds floating upon it. As Charlotte looked at the ocean scenery through the full length windows that made up the far side of the house, she shook her head in amazed disbelief that she felt so comfortable here.

After all, this was the house that Phineas had shared with Raven. Charlotte never thought that she could be comfortable moving into the space that once belonged to Raven, but one couldn't argue with the value of Los Angeles real estate. This house was worth at least five million dollars and because of the sheer number of years that Raven had lived, there was no mortgage remaining. It had been placed in her name and Phineas', a little technicality that would one day have to be taken care of, but for now, neither Charlotte, nor Phineas brought up the subject. It would be sheer insanity to ask Raven to sign over the deed to Phineas and trying to deal with the legalities of explaining how either one could be still alive considering when the home was purchased would just be too difficult to prove.

As Charlotte took off her sweater and went to the kitchen to pour herself a glass of iced tea from the refrigerator, she mused that some things were best left alone. It had always been Phineas' house too, and who was she to argue that he should move? Maybe she was even a little proud of the fact that someone as handsome as Phineas had chosen her. And if she really admitted the truth to herself, the danger he possessed was a bit of a turn on. He had never shown any form of violence toward her, but if provoked she knew that he had the capabilities to protect her from harm.

"Phin?" she called out to no answer. She sat down on the couch, sipping her tea, relieved for a few minutes to herself. She surmised that Phineas must have gone out for a quick surfing session or maybe even for a flight. She didn't like to think of the times that he shifted into bird form, but she also knew that it was wrong to deny him of who he really was. Sometimes he needed to fly just to get away from it all. At least that's what he would tell her. She wondered, however, if he wasn't doing it sometimes to try and communicate with Raven.

She reached for her glass and took another sip, but choked on the cool liquid when Phineas' voice surprised her. "Hey! When did you get in?"

"Gosh, you scared me. I didn't hear you," she said, getting up from the couch and doing a running jump into his arms. She collided into him relishing the feel of his strong chest, longing for his arms to wrap around her. Instead, he held her at arm's length and then gently put his hands on her shoulders and sat her back onto the couch.

"Everything okay?" she asked.

"I was taking a nap," he said pointing to the bedroom.

"You were taking a nap?" she asked incredulously. "You barely need sleep."

As a demon gypsy, Phineas had been brought back to life after sustaining a fatal gunshot wound to the chest. Raven had nurtured him and then taught him necessities of ever-lasting life. Specifically, how to shift into bird form, tap into powers of mind control, and most importantly, how to yield strength from the elements. Sleep was for humans and the weak.

For birds and demon gypsies, sleep was something to do when there was nothing better to do, or when the darkness would make hunting for food too difficult. But Phineas and Raven had stronger eyesight than an average bird and for them, the night was their preferred time for feeding. There was a freedom that came with the darkness. The ability to shift back and forth from bird form to human without risk of being noticed was intoxicating. Why sleep when there were so many better things to do? It was that thought process that made them succumb only for a mere three hours a day.

"Headache," he said off-handedly, and then as if to emphasize his words, his hand went to pinch the bridge of his nose as his eyes closed trying to stave off the pain that coursed through him.

"Again?" The worry in Charlotte's voice was evident. She had never known Phineas to display any form of weakness.

"It's probably just some...something."

"Well, that explains it," she joked. "Maybe it's bird flu," she added, trying her best to continue a light-hearted tone to a subject that obviously worried him.

"Don't worry," he crossed the room and brought her into his arms. "It's not something. I'm sure it's nothing."

"Well, thanks for explaining it so clearly. But, since you keep getting these headaches, do you think you should see a doctor?"

"How would you suggest I explain things when they go to take my vitals? Resting heartbeat. Pulse. Not to mention that I'd have a hell of a time explaining the fact that I'm a few hundred years old. They would send me straight into a psyche ward or a lab for extreme testing."

"You don't have to tell them your real age."

"Yeah, that would be the least of their concerns," he smiled, trying his best to diminish any worry that plagued his fiancee. He loved her and the last thing he wanted her to know was that he had been getting messages from Raven, each one more urgent than the last.

"I know it's something else. You can tell me." Charlotte studied him, unable to shake her intuition.

"You're sure?"

Charlotte ran her hand soothingly up the back of his neck. "Of course. Just tell me."

He loved her touch. It made him feel loved...even human. He trusted her implicitly because she had trusted him even after Samantha's horrible accident. It was an incident that he had never wanted to occur, but he wasn't completely innocent in his involvement. Raven had ironically been the first to encourage his relationship with Charlotte. He never expected to have fallen so head over heels in love with her and he thanked his lucky stars that she had been able to overlook his past with Raven. Maybe she would still.

"I've been getting messages from Raven. It's causing me the headaches."

"What?! Well, she is one big headache. No wonder you've been feeling sick. Just tell her to take a flying leap and leave you alone."

"Charlotte, don't mince words."

"I'm serious, Phin. I hate what she did to us...all of us. To Samantha, but also to you all those years. To Suki. To James. There isn't one of us that hasn't been affected by her treachery."

"She seems scared," Phineas interrupted, not addressing her tirade. "She talks about losing control of the Romani Realms."

"What difference does that make?" Charlotte asked. She knew that she sounded insensitive, and Raven had after all saved Phineas, but that didn't excuse what she had attempted against Samantha or herself for that matter.

"If she loses control of the masses in the Romani Realms, she may be trapped there forever...and not just trapped, but without her right mind."

In spite of her love for Phineas, Charlotte couldn't hide her real emotions. It was too soon since everything had gone down in the Romani Realms. Not enough time had passed for her to forget the risk they took in going there to save Samantha when her life hung in the balance between the real world and the purgatory that was the Realms. Without stopping to think, she sent Phineas a "whatever" look.

"Listen Charlotte, I know you must think I'm crazy for caring...considering...everything..." he said searching for the right word or phrase, but then deciding better of it. "But..."

"But nothing, Phin. It's just a ploy," Charlotte insisted.

"Listen Charlotte, I chose you. I'm here with you."

She nodded, uneasiness filling her as she instinctively knew the conversation wasn't over and wasn't going exactly as she hoped.

"But..." Phineas continued... "If Raven is trapped there it means that her powers are compromised. Powers that I will always rely on. She is older and more powerful than I am. She still supplies me with a lifeblood."

Suddenly, Charlotte's eyes widened. "Are you telling me that if something affects her, it affects you?"

Phineas nodded gravely. "If she dies, I die."

"Phin, no." Charlotte's eyes immediately filled with tears. "I just want to go back to the way it was when we first came back from that place. We were safe, happy. We talked about our future."

Her words were tumbling out, faster and more frantic as her emotions took over. Phineas leaned over and kissed her on the forehead. "Just breathe," he said and held her closely. "We'll work this out."

"You promise?"

"I'm going to go out for a beach run. Don't worry. I promise that everything will be okay."

Charlotte watched Phineas leave, a nervousness washing over her. She paced the room once and poured herself another glass of tea, but no sooner set it down, not able to swallow the sweet liquid. She flipped on the television, but after scanning the channels, she shut it off again.

Finally, she retreated to the bedroom and there in the closet on the top shelf was a shoebox, which contained something she knew would calm her ragged nerves. She pulled down the box and audibly exhaled as she pulled open the lid, seeing something that always gave her hope and filled her with joy. It was a sketch done in charcoal of a little girl that looked just like her.

"Shadow." Charlotte spoke the name of the girl she had met in the Romani Realms – the girl who was destined to be the future daughter of she and Phineas.

# # #

Chapter Four

A middle aged woman dressed in a sophisticated brocade dress banged a gavel on a long, rectangular oak desk. Seated around the desk were two other women and three men of similar age and based on their clothing, what seemed to be of similar social status.

"The monthly meeting of the Romani Realms Council is officially called to order. Let it be recorded that all members are here and accounted for."

"Here," repeated the gathered crowd said in unison.

"Without further ado, we will continue with discussions of last month's most pressing issue. Specifically, what to do about the diminishing resources of innocents within our Realms. Howard, do you care to start with your State of the Union Report."

The man seated to her left had just popped what looked like a beetle into his mouth. After chewing quite loudly for a good minute, and receiving numerous eye rolls from the other women, he answered.

"Myra, thank you. I'd be happy to comply," he cleared his throat, shuffled his papers and then finally, putting on a deep baritone, began to speak.

"As commissioner of security for the Romani Realms' upper class elite, I have developed a proposal to ration the feeding of our lower class system."

"Ration?" one woman questioned. "Do you mean we only feed them on certain days or do you mean we limit their diet to a more meager substance?"

"Excellent question, Talia. I suggest we proceed with the recruitment of more innocents while simultaneously limiting the general population's feeding of such people."

The man seated across from Howard, a skinny fellow named Burl, rolled up his shirtsleeves to reveal scars across each wrist, and immediately crossed his arms in an effort to hide his weakness. "I'm not sure I understand the connection," he said. "If we successfully recruit more innocents then why do we have to also restrict the diet of the lower classes?"

"Let me backtrack," Howard suggested. "The Romani Realms are somewhat similar to a third world country – poverty stricken and desolate for the majority of our inhabitants. But a few privileged members of the society," he motioned around the table with a flourish, "lead a different lifestyle."

"Thank God," Myra joked to which Talia also tittered and laughed.

"I'll continue," Howard added. "I obviously don't need to preach about our need to maintain our current lifestyle. We enjoy the best food, wine, and accommodations."

"Well yes, but it is rather annoying that as Council Members we have to purchase our luxury and splendor," Myra interrupted.

"Yes Howard, can't something be done about that? I mean, Myra is right. Shouldn't the elite members of society be immune from having to make purchases?" Talia inquired.

"If by 'purchases' you mean our barter system, well...that's all we're set up for. I've been in the Romani Realms for nearly half a century and money was long decided to be worthless here, but our recent system of providing innocents to ward off the condition of soullessness has been quite effective."

"But? Burl prompted. "I hear there aren't enough to go around and the soulless ones are getting restless."

Howard continued. "That does seem to be the talk. Our top commodity – innocent souls – is growing scare."

"I guess that's what happens when you feed on them," Myra said matter of factly.

"True. One can only ingest innocents for so long before the one partaking of that..." Howard struggled for the right word, "crime...pays the price with their own soul. It becomes a vicious circle. We ingest the innocents in order to obtain their outlook toward life, but the very act takes portions of their soul until every innocent bit is used up. Not to mention that the act of feeding ends up robbing us of our humanity."

"Oh I don't believe that last bit," Myra spoke up. "I've been eating them for years and I'm the same as I always was."

"Myra, may I remind you that you were sent to the Realms for multiple reasons: tax evasion, robbing seniors of their pension, insider trading, and even black market slave trade," Howard said, reviewing his notes. "You were hardly innocent when you arrived so how the ability to recognize whether you have lost any of your innocence is probably like looking for a dropped earring on a sandy beach."

Myra rolled her eyes and tutted her tongue. "You would have done the same in my position. And, I wouldn't have been caught if that stupid maid of mine hadn't gotten so damned nosey. She should end up here. And then that court expected me to rot in jail for fifteen years?! That was absurd. Suicide was a much better option and the fact that I had never gone to church or temple a day in my life is ironically what saved me."

Myra turned to Talia and whispered conspiratorially. "I knew that would be the case. Without heaven to claim me, my body gets to live on here. And, it's not so bad now, is it?"

"Now that we've gotten rid of that bossy boots Raven," Myra said with her nose in the air. "She always had such an air about her, but I knew that having such a young thing on the council was not a good idea. Didn't I tell you?"

Myra raised her eyebrows in confusion. "But she's centuries old. That's the problem. Her history with this place, being able to come and go as she pleases, that freaky shapeshifting thing she does..." Myra shook her head as if truly troubled.

Talia placed a hand on her friend's arm. "Don't let it get to you. She won't harm us. She can't. We are untouchable."

Myra laughed and waved her hand in the air to brush away the ridiculousness of the thought. "Oh I never worried about her. I'm just so damned jealous of her skin..so supple." She smacked her lips as if she wished she could feed on Raven. "It feels good to stick it to her where it counts. Let her eat turnips for awhile. It's never a good thing to allow one person too much control. I, for one, am glad that we've removed her from power. More for us."

At that comment, Howard cleared his throat and looked pointedly at the two women who now wielded the most control of the Realms. "Ladies, may we continue our discussion?"

"Please," Myra said with a flourish.

"Rumors have surfaced that the soulless people trapped in the Realms have taken notice of the disparity between the classes. As you know, the classes, which in addition to having access to very different lifestyles, also have one notable difference."

The others seated around the table nodded, knowing what Howard spoke of even before he continued. "The lower class are those who have lost control of their souls while we, the upper class, still maintain a portion of our humanity. Mind you, I do hope I am not offending anyone by saying 'a portion'. I merely point out the fact that if we continue to feed on others, eventually we too will lose our souls. Our system is somewhat flawed," he said as an after thought. "Perhaps change is needed."

There was silence around the table until the other man, a tall gentleman named Burl, who kept two switchblades in his pockets at all times, finally spoke up. "Howard, has that last point actually been proven? Do we really know that by feeding on innocents, our morality...and I use that term loosely...will leave us? I mean, they are tempting to us in the same way that others view alcohol, drugs, even sugar. There can't be a problem with that."

"But those are all addictive entities," Howard persevered. "Certainly we aren't prone to such *animal* tendencies."

Burl pulled out one of his switchblades, made a small incision in his pinky finger and then started to suck his blood as he thought of an appropriate comeback. He closed his eyes, savoring the flavor of his own internal liquid before continuing. "Maintaining a lavish lifestyle comes with a price. Every bit of comfort, any special food item such as cake or even coffee – something one considers a way of life in the regular world – has to be paid for and here, it is with one's own innocence."

"Don't be ridiculous!" Myra spoke up. "That would be miserable for us. Why would we do that?"

"At least you still have some semblance of feelings and emotions to recognize it as such," Howard added. "I'm not sure I agree...or disagree. Hmm, interesting. Lately, nothing seems to matter."

The others looked at Howard as he gazed into space. The realization that one of their own was starting to lose his mind, nearly becoming the same as the soulless ones, was a startling revelation – one that the others never wanted to consider or endure themselves.

Burl broke the sudden silence. "If the loss of innocence eventually leads to a warped mind, so be it. I for one, am willing to take my chances. For all I know, I've already reached criminal status," he pounded the table and started to laugh to which others around the table joined in, the tension of moments earlier now broken.

Myra pounded her gavel once more. "I think we've heard enough to allow us to vote. Do we have a motion on the table?"

Howard raised his hand. "I think Raven had a point and that we should do as she was attempting...to maintain the supply of innocents. We must limit our own lifestyles for the greater good – to ensure that morality among those with souls continues to thrive."

Myra spoke: "All those in favor, say 'I'."

With the exception of Howard, silence filled the air. "Very well. All those who reject the proposal and wish to continue living as an elite group, feeding as we desire, and enjoying our natural resources, say 'Nay'."

"Nay," the others around the table repeated.

The gavel pounded with a heavy thud. "The Council has spoken. Our next order of business: to recruit the innocent that will fulfill the Triad." Myra looked around the table. "I hear she is coming soon."

"What does that mean?" Howard asked in a worried tone.

"This one innocent will be able to feed our souls for what will feel like an eternity!" Myra beamed.

"Oh Myra! We must get her. We must!" Talia had stood up from her seat and was pacing frantically.

"Calm down, Talia. All in good time," Myra soothed. "First we must make sure that she is a rightful third of the Triad. Raven had spoken about this and led us to believe that she controlled the Triad, although...," Myra smiled with amusement, "we know that was just wishful thinking on her part."

"It was that genie, wasn't it?" Burl inquired.

Myra nodded. "Yes, but the privilege can be passed onto her Releasors. The one called Samantha seems to be willing to join our community. I say we welcome her with open arms."

# # #

Chapter Five

The minute Charlotte arrived, Suki's intuition went into high gear.

"Something's off with you...I can tell." Suki looked at Charlotte with the concern of a mother, although in spite of being 350-years-old, she didn't look beyond late twenties and her long, wavy locks and soulful brown eyes always managed to turn heads. That, and the fact that she was somewhat vain, caused Suki to prefer to think of herself as a hipper, cooler aunt or even a big sister.

She tossed off the high-heeled shoes that she always wore over flats because for one, they made her legs look longer; and two, her true love, James, a Shade who had watched over her throughout time said seeing her legs in heels made him want to follow her anywhere she wanted to go.

Never one to lament about her own problems, Charlotte replied, "It's nothing."

"Charlotte, you've got a hitch in your giddy-up. Now spill it."

"It's Phineas."

"And?"

"And Raven."

"Shut the back door!" Samantha shouted, hearing the tail end of the conversation as she entered Suki's penthouse condo.

Suki patted the couch next to her, indicating that Samantha should join them. "Charlotte was just going to tell me what's got her so worried."

"In a nutshell, he's been getting these really bad migraines and he thinks it's Raven," Charlotte said.

"That figures. That girl is a total headache," Samantha said with a flip of her hair.

"Yeah, well, that girl is also still connected to him apparently," Charlotte added.

"What do you mean?" Samantha asked, leaning forward, her brow furrowing.

"He thinks something's wrong in the Romani Realms and basically, if anything happens to Raven, it affects him too. Should she die, he'll die."

Suki sat silently, but the fact that she was slowly nodding her head gave Charlotte cause to worry. She could tell that Phineas had spoken the truth.

Suki wore a grave expression – her alliances clearly divided. Charlotte and Samantha were her responsibility and Phineas, while previously aligned with Raven, had inadvertently caused Samantha to end up in the Romani Realms in the first place. But his love for Charlotte was evident and he proved his loyalty to her when they launched the rescue mission last year. It was a mission that nearly cost all of them their lives, but they came back from the Realms – that is, all of them except Daniel, the man who Samantha had fallen in love with and seemed to be the only good thing about that place. The sorrow that grew in the Romani Realms never seemed to disappear and now, even when they were safely back in Los Angeles, it threatened their existence.

Charlotte continued, "What would I do if something happened to him, Suki? It's not just for me, but..." she patted her stomach. It was known that Phineas and Charlotte's future child had been introduced to them in the Romani Realms and clearly they both quickly felt the protective parental instincts. "I can't lose him or we'll never conceive Shadow," Charlotte said referring to the little girl who resembled her so remarkably.

"You won't," Suki reassured. She rubbed Charlotte's back and smiled when the girl rested her head against her shoulder. "Phineas will figure something out. I'll talk to James as well. After all, he's had experience with Raven too."

As much as she hated to think about it, she couldn't escape the truth that James had been involved with Raven before Suki had even met him. It was one reason that Raven had developed a hatred for her, although how could she have known? If there was one thing that could place a divide between women, it was a man.

\# \# \#

Chapter Six

Daniel was what the Romani Realms referred to as "a necessary allowance." Long ago, in the real world, he worked as a mediator. Although he preferred his "day job" as a farmer and found his ability to barter goods to be a saving grace, he had an important side business. He was the only person in the Romani Realms to still make use of the skill set he had employed in the real world.

His continuing ability to work as a mediator was an important characteristic to possess in a world where violence quickly broke out. He had proven not to be an extremist, which was what the high counsel had originally feared when he arrived. A mediator was one who most likely wanted everyone to get along and play nicely in the sandbox. But Daniel knew that such a life was a fantasy in the Realms. Violence was a necessary outlet for the soulless ones. Not only did he recognize this fact, he knew when to step in and mediate...and when to leave people to their own devices.

Raven came up behind him as he worked at the kitchen table on a brief that was presented to him by the high counsel. She rubbed his tense shoulders and smiled as he immediately relaxed under her tender touch. "You seem stressed," she noted, ironic as it may seem to make a comment like that considering where they resided.

"Some days I find it harder to keep my sanity," he said.

"Don't say that. I would die if you weren't you."

They had this discussion before. Daniel's "talent" for knowing when to allow the high counsel to feed on the minds of the soulless ones, taking advantage of their fleeting innocence. And, he knew when to step in. It was a delicate path to walk. He feared that in doing so, it wore down a bit of his own soul every time he looked the other way. "It kills me to be working for them, considering we have to hide you. But, it's the best way for me to keep an ear to the ground and know what they have planned."

"I know that. You don't think I'm questioning you? I trust you, Daniel. More than anyone."

He looked up and like so many days before, he was amazed at what he now saw in her. Purity. Strength. A woman who had so much taken from her, but had survived and was better for it.

"Raven, I've never told anyone my fears...not even Samantha because she was an innocent. Everyone thinks that's appealing, but here...in this place...," he paused. "I know that I need a partner who understands me and what I've been through, *what I do*." He said these last words not much louder than a whisper as if even he couldn't bear to admit the truth to himself.

Raven nodded, understanding what he meant. Wanting to reassure him, she spoke in a quiet but firm voice. "You do what you need to do and that doesn't make you like them. Your quiet existence is the only way to survive this hell." She sat down next to him and took his hand.

"I need you too. I feel like taking care of you is something I was meant to do."

She smiled. "There was a time when I would never have let a man take care of me...or even think that he could."

"You're talking about Phineas."

She nodded. "I was older. I gave him life. It was never a relationship that started on equal footing, but it grew into a comfortable one. But...comfortable isn't really what you want in a relationship, is it?"

"I suppose not." His eyes met her gaze. There was no denying that something was brewing between them. Furthermore, he would never describe the way his heart pounded out of control when she was near as comfortable. The tension between them was anything but, which is perhaps why Raven continued to talk, not daring to let their eyes stay on each other too long.

"I still feel responsible for him...and Daniel, I've tried to contact him. I wanted you to know."

"I understand."

"If something happens to me...it affects him."

"Don't. You don't have to explain. I know what it means for both of you. We all have our past," he said without going into details about his own. He rubbed the top of her hand with his thumb, moving in small back and forth motions against her smooth and creamy skin. "You got a bad rap, you know that?"

She tossed her head back and laughed at the unexpected comment. "I think that's the nicest thing anyone has ever said to me."

To show her appreciation, she leaned toward him, her eyes meeting his once more, but sensing that Daniel wanted to lean in for something more, she quickly threw her arms around his neck for a hug and then just as quickly separated.

"I'm going to make a cup of tea. Do you want one?"

Daniel nodded, and returned to his work. He watched Raven step into the kitchen, admiring her slight, but curvaceous frame. He may be safe with the counsel, but Raven was a different story. They say that the higher one sits, the harder they fall. She didn't care about having to forgo her political power, but she certainly wasn't prepared to lose her gypsy powers, which was something the council was trying to plot.

She was in a dangerous situation and the fact that Daniel was falling for her meant that his situation was just as precarious.

# # #

Chapter Seven

J ames presided over his bar like a captain of a
ship. The staff respected him and worked their
hardest, not one slacker was among them. They also
admired him, some more than others.

"James...you look delicious," a waitress with
platinum blonde hair purred as she walked by,
tapping a finger to her lips.

He gave her a surprised, but appreciative smile.

"Don't let it go to your head." Suki's voice caught
him by surprise. He turned to find her just entering
the bar. As usual, her timing was impeccable.

"I have no idea what that was about," he said
innocently.

"It probably has to do with the smear of chocolate
that's gracing your lower lip."

James turned to look in the large mirror that
hung above the bar. Indeed, the sample of chocolate
mousse that his chef had prepared still lingered. He
reached a hand toward his mouth, but Suki was fast,
appearing next to him instantly in a show of
supernatural prowess. She planted her hands on
either side of his face and kissed his lips hard and
fast. And as he responded, leaning into her, she

instinctively knew she was being watched and opened her own eyes to glare at the waitress who would certainly never make that same mistake again.

When she released James, he noticed the girl scuttling away into the kitchen. "What did you do?"

"Me? Nothing!"

"Suki?"

She rolled her eyes skyward and looked sufficiently guilty. "I loved you?"

"And?"

"And, I gave her the evil eye."

James looked amused. "What does that entail?"

Suki gave him the same dirty look that she spied on the waitress, a look that said 'hands off or else'!

"That is one freakin' scary look. When did you learn to do that?"

"I just developed it when I saw her hungry look. It actually made me lose my appetite," Suki said in her proper Southern accent.

"I love you," James said, pulling her close. "You and your jealous ways."

"I don't have jealous ways," she protested.

"Show me a woman who doesn't possess jealousy and I'll take it back."

Suki remained quiet, knowing that he had her with that one.

"I need to check on an order...in there," James craned his neck toward the kitchen.

Suki raised her eyebrows, knowing that the hot waitress who had eyes for her own hottie was still in there. "Well, go on then. I'll prove that I don't have a jealous bone in my body. Not even my little finger," she said, twirling her last finger in front of her face.

"Here, I'll be back in a flash and then we can enjoy our night," he said, pulling out a chair for her.

He went back behind the bar and was just walking toward the kitchen when Suki called out. "James!"

He turned with a 'you've got to be kidding me' expression. She knew that he immediately thought she really was a jealous crazy, so without saying a word, Suki merely pointed at the mirror. It was explanation enough.

The massive mirror was more than a decorative fixture. It was the portal that transported James and Suki into the Romani Realms last year. But without them calling upon its powers, it started to ripple on its own as James walked past, yet it stopped the moment he glanced at it.

The mirror wasn't just a one-way ticket into the Romani Realms. It was also a conduit into other times as well. James regularly used it to visit London during the Industrial Revolution when businesses were in full swing, including his building company, a promising establishment that leveraged the power of steam. It afforded him to live a lifestyle in Los Angeles that he enjoyed, overseeing his restaurant and bar in the same building where Suki lived. It kept him close to her so that he could serve as her Shade – her protector.

"Has it ever done that before?"

James shook his head and peered closer, but maintaining a stealth like stance should the pull of the elements suddenly force him within the portal. Looking carefully, he could see the trapped souls that tried to gain a foothold into the present realm when the mirror's portal would open. There was always one or two that would attempt it, but the powers in charge would force them back into submission and keep them from escaping the Romani Realms where the elite class used them. James never liked power mongers, but he couldn't argue that in their condition the soulless ones couldn't simply be let loose on the earth.

And just as soon as the rippling had started, it ceased.

"Is it over?"

"Well, whatever 'it' was," he said, staring back at the mirror once more, inspecting its shiny glass, but only seeing his own reflection staring back.

# # #

Chapter Eight

If an uprising broke out within the Romani Realms it would be of no surprise to Daniel. In fact, he would never admit this to anyone, but privately he couldn't understand how the issue that was at the heart of the matter hadn't surfaced years ago. Countries had fought for power; people had fought for freedom; but here, in the Romani Realms the one thing worth fighting for was the ability to feel. What's more, the soulless ones were determined to make those on top feel.

The Council lived in blissful unawareness of their desire, too absorbed in their own day to day extravagances. Although he could bring the topic up with the Council and even offer his mediation services to alleviate the growing issue, he remained quiet. He had learned that in the Romani Realms the tendency was to shoot the messenger and he had enough issues maintaining his favor and staying out of trouble with those in control.

On the one occasion that he had broached the subject just to see what the reaction would be his words were met with incredulous disbelief. "What do the soulless ones expect?" Burl had spatted.

"They certainly don't want to feel! That can't be the truth," Myra added with a confused tone. "I don't think those types have the ability to comprehend what that privilege would do to their lives. Why, it would destroy them."

The Council then preached about their innate right to hold onto their emotions and that this did not apply to the soulless ones. They didn't see that this attitude made their land ripe for an uprising.

If successful in their quest, the soulless ones would feel as much as the ruling class...they would be equal. And that was something that the ruling class just wouldn't tolerate. The Romani Realms were about to experience a change and the world's balance between good and evil would be altered.

With dramatic change on the horizon, Daniel feared irreversible effects, but was powerless to help. For that matter, both sides had so many flaws that he wouldn't know who to step up for and so he remained quiet, taking care of himself and Raven. Although he knew in doing so, he also showed flaws.

Having the ability to feel was as much a joy as it was a burden. Had Daniel not been able to share his emotions with Samantha, and now with Raven, it would have killed him to live with the memories that brought him to the Romani Realms. Now, they were becoming more distant.

Any memories, even those created in the Romani Realms, could be dangerous. Daniel had managed to bury some relating to Samantha, either due to his own defense mechanisms or because he truly had fallen in love with Raven. But now he realized that loving Raven once again placed him in a precarious position.

The soulless ones fed on the emotions of the innocents that were thrown to them. But everyone knew that the ration of innocents was growing scare. The Council would either need to find new recruits or others who had special abilities that were appealing...people like Raven.

Feeding on someone like her would provide enough emotional charge, almost like a battery, to last the soulless ones for years to come. The risk in taking Raven was great because of her powers, and Daniel hoped that fact would help to keep her safe. Otherwise, it would become a slippery slope with each Council member then turning on the other in order to partake of "an exceptional food source."

Daniel could imagine them turning on each other, hijacking each other when least expected. For now, he kept this horrible thought contained. He shuddered wondering how the idea occurred to him and worried what the implications meant for his own humanity.

Like so many times since Raven had turned up at his place needing protection, he found himself experiencing disturbing dreams and even during waking times, his thoughts bordered on the macabre. He inhaled deeply, smelling the scent of lavender that grew outside his bedroom window. It comforted him and helped him forget...something. Something that was just out of reach of his memories, but he knew in his gut was a worry. The closer he became to Raven, the more he feared that something dark lurked within himself. It seemed that he saw more purity in her each day and as he came to realize her true nature, reflections of his own humanity somehow disturbed him.

The early morning sun was rising higher in the sky. It was unusual for him to still be in bed, but today he wasn't in a hurry to get on with his chores. He had tried unsuccessfully to fall back asleep when his worrisome thoughts bothered him. Having been unsuccessful for the better part of two hours, now he was just too tired to rise.

He turned on his side to find that Raven was still sleeping soundly beside him. She had taken to sleeping in his bed for no reason other than her own protection. Both of them felt better knowing the other was nearby and for the last few months just being near each other was enough. Until it wasn't.

Their confessionals had served to bring them closer together. The talks also made Raven that much more attractive to Daniel. Emotions and feelings that he had buried now reared their head, along with other parts of his anatomy. In the past few days, he had retreated from bed in favor of a cold shower, but today he just had no interest in leaving.

He gently lifted the covers to peek at her perfect form. He thought maybe one look would suffice his cravings for her and give him the strength to carry the image with him for the rest of the day once he left her side. It wasn't enough today. It only made him want her more. A throbbing need pulsed through him more than he had ever known.

He recalled the times of late that he had watched her when she wasn't aware of it. When she bent down to pick vegetables exposing her ample cleavage. When she reached for something on the top shelf, making her dress rise above her thighs. When she left the bath dressed only in a towel, he imagined what she would look like should it drop. And now, as he peered underneath the thin sheet, she lay with her legs slightly apart and he wanted more than anything to reach between them.

He had shown her respect for months, not wanting to hurry their relationship, but his self control was faltering. He reached beneath the sheet to stroke himself, unable to deter his desirous thoughts. His movement was next to nothing, but she stirred and then turned to face him.

"You're still here," she yawned lazily.

"Um, yeah, I really need to get going," he said, but given his physical condition, he resisted getting out of bed, not wanting her to know how she affected him.

Raven rolled over on her side and eyed Daniel. Something was different. He was normally up at the crack of dawn and of late, he would jump from the bed the moment she stirred as if avoiding her. She furrowed her brow, trying to figure him out.

"Those crops aren't going to harvest themselves. So lazy bones, no life of luxury for you. Go on," she teased and then poked a finger into his ribs for good measure. Daniel immediately recoiled, his secret of being extremely ticklish now exposed. "You're ticklish!" Raven squealed with delight and then proceeded to dig her fingers from both hands into his sides.

"Raven stop...stop it!" Daniel screamed as best he could between his gasping laughter. But his mock dismay only served to make Raven more playful. She jumped on top of him, straddling her legs on either side of his waist to try and pin him down and tickle him mercilessly. That's when she discovered that Daniel had been hiding another reaction beyond his ticklish nerves.

Her eyes opened wider. "Oh my god, I'm so sorry. Uhh, good morning?"

"Get off," he replied more seriously.

Raven raised her eyebrow, suddenly coquettish. She too had been watching Daniel for weeks. He was beyond kind to her, which was more appealing than even his handsome good looks. She had been shy around him for months, not wanting to go into a territory that was beyond their friendship, but at this moment she couldn't escape the thought of what it would be like to be with him under different circumstances. "Do you really mean that? Because you don't seem like you really mean that."

"I do. Now."

Raven moved her hand away from Daniel's ribs and lowered them to the area that was protruding upwards.

"Raven..."

"Why are you keeping this all to yourself?" she asked softly.

He shrugged. "I didn't want you to feel uncomfortable."

"So...how long has this been going on?"

"Every morning for over a month," he admitted.

"Really?" she was more than pleased.

"You sound surprised."

"I'm just amazed that you have those feelings. Considering this, you're the one who must be uncomfortable." She paused, weighing which direction she wanted the conversation to go. It didn't take long to decide.

"In fact, I bet it would get really uncomfortable if I did this." Raven pressed her hips toward his manhood and leaned her ample breasts forward giving him a view of her beautiful figure.

Daniel closed his eyes and took a deep breath, still trying to maintain some semblance of control. "I just don't think it's a good idea. You need to stay here for your own safety and if we get involved beyond our current situation and you decide that it isn't good for you, then it can get messy."

"Or uncomfortable," she joked.

"Yes, that too."

But Raven knew how to get what she wanted and at that moment she wanted Daniel. She bent her head down to him and placed her lips on his, still keeping her legs on either side of him, relishing in the feel of his reaction.

"I can't help it," she said innocently. "I know you tried to hide this, but now that I know...I just want you to make love to me."

"You say that now, but..." he looked at her face, so beautiful in the morning light.

"Daniel, I've seen you look at me," she said. Daring him not to look right then, she lifted her top for a teasing glance. "I know you want me."

Daniel may have been the most moral person in the Romani Realms. He had thought of the consequences of living with Raven and being involved. For more times than he cared to remember, he had taken cold showers or gone out to work the land in order to not think of her body. But he was also a man and he could no longer curb his instincts toward her.

Raven craved his touch. Now that she knew he felt the same, the knowledge that they would be together filled her completely. Reading her thoughts, Daniel reached for her waist and flipped her over. Raven may have been supernatural, but he was the one to gain the upper hand as he positioned himself above her.

# # #

Chapter Nine

S uki awoke to discover that James wasn't beside her. She meandered into the kitchen, smelling the morning coffee and hoping that he would be seated at the table, but even before she reached the room, she knew that something was amiss.

The coffee had been brewed and one cup sat alone in the sink. Her own favorite mug sat next to the coffee maker with a pitcher of cream beside it, waiting. She poured herself a cup and paced the kitchen, knowing that James had felt the strange pull of energy just as she had. The incident at the bar was connected to Charlotte's dilemma with Raven and even Samantha's restless desire to return to the Romani Realms. There was trouble afoot.

Unable to relax, she emptied the coffee from her mug into a to-go cup before returning to the bedroom to get dressed and go in search of the man she loved.

# # #

The bar was empty at this early hour of the morning. The staff had another two hours before they were required to show, but Suki had been right in thinking she would find James here. She entered the bar's main room from a door located off of her building's lobby. The exclusive bar had gotten its reputation for being akin to an old-fashioned speakeasy partly because of its creative entrance – a door that was practically hidden from view due to the striped wallpaper that masked its appearance. Under James' direction he had created one of the most popular bars in the area simply by recalling his own past.

It took a minute for Suki to adjust her eyes to the dim lighting inside. The ambiance also hid her presence from James who was staring into the same mirror that troubled them last night.

"It's no wonder the girls who encounter you are doomed. Even you can't take your eyes off yourself," she quipped.

He turned, surprised to hear her voice at the early hour. His green eyes danced and the light in them matched the beam of his smile. "I had an eyelash stuck in my eye," he lied.

Moving closer to him with catlike grace, Suki leaned her forehead against his. "Hmm, I think I see it. Let me help you..."

He pulled her in close to kiss her a proper good morning. James could deliver the kind of kiss that makes a girl's heart thump, but even after a year of being with him, it still felt like the first time...every time.

"Look at that," he said against her mouth, "I'm all better. I just needed to close my eyes and let it wash away."

"Happy to oblige you, kind sir," she whispered back.

"So my little genie...I expected you to be sipping your coffee in bed, wearing that nightie that I hated to drag myself away from."

"Then why did you?" she asked, although she suspected the answer before it came. "Can I convince you to come back upstairs?"

"You know there's nothing I would rather do, but I need to use this time in a more prudent manner. I'm going to take a quick trip to visit Maybelline," he motioned to the mirror portal. "I told Kate that I was going to be coming in late today. You remember her, my general manager? Anyway, she offered to handle things while I'm gone."

"I bet she did." Suki raised her eyebrows, not liking the fact that James had delivered news of his impending departure to a buxom blonde before telling her.

"Every time I'm with you it's too amazing to ruin with news of me leaving," he said, nuzzling her ear lobe, taking it in between his teeth and giving it a light tug.

Shivers erupted over her arms and spine and she instantly forgave him. "Do you think Maybelline can help?"

Like Suki, Maybelline was born in the South and had a strong belief that children needed structure, roots and discipline. Truth be told, James was a tad bit afraid of her commanding presence, but over the years they had developed a sort of supernatural partnership. Maybelline had taken care of him after his father died, but she was now much more than his mammy. She was the only other person he had ties to and the one who could pull him back to the present from other realms. Much in the way that Raven and Phineas would forever be connected, so was James to Maybelline.

In answer to Suki's question, he simply said, "I'm just hoping she might have an explanation for this uneasy feeling I can't shake."

Suki nodded, feeling the same nervousness. "I know what you mean. I've been feeling like a cat thrown into a burlap sack, all claws and anxiety without any good explanation for it. Maybe Maybelline can give her old world magic a spin and can feel the pulse of the spirits from the other realms," she suggested.

"That's what I'm hoping for. I've been feeling this weird pull for a few weeks and ignored it, but yesterday...some entity was trying to use our portal to get here and I just can't let that happen. Not when I've got you to watch over," he said, tickling her under her chin.

After giving her a peck on the cheek, James grabbed his backpack and hauled it over his shoulder and then turned to face the mirror.

Placing a hand on his arm, Suki found it hard to say goodbye. Portals were always risky ways of travel, even for a Shade. "Can I come?" Suki tried, knowing what his answer would be.

James turned to glance over his shoulder at Suki and offered her the best answer he could think of to calm and reassure her. James pulled her in, wrapping his arms around the small circle of her waist. "I think this is a trip I best make alone. I'll be back soon."

Suki nodded, and then put on a brave face. It wouldn't do James any good if he was worrying about her back here. "I'll be fine. But, maybe you can get Maybelline to make me a sweet potato pie?"

"You make the whip cream and I'll bring back the pie."

"Deal."

"I'll be back by tomorrow night."

# # #

Chapter Ten

With every other lover, Raven's sexual experiences had been characterized by frenzy – the tearing of clothes and an animalistic need to be satiated. She felt a deep desire for Daniel, but also something new...tenderness. Also an ocean of need to show him what he taught her about herself – that this was her real nature.

"I love you, Daniel," she said looking up at him. He was positioned above her, his body between her legs, but the two would-be lovers had yet to become one. It was important to her that she say what was on her mind before anything further occurred.

He gently brushed a strand of hair from her eyes, and let his thumb caress the side of her cheek. For a moment he just stared back at her, but never did she fear her feelings weren't returned for Daniel looked into her eyes so deeply and with so much love in his expression, his lashes even lightly tinged with tears.

"You make me happy, Raven," he finally found his voice. "I never would have thought it was possible to feel so much in this place, but I feel love for you beyond anything I ever expected."

"I've waited a lifetime for you," then she laughed in spite of trying to convey a serious conversation. "Actually, it's more like the equivalent of four lifetimes. And in all that time, I've never found anyone as perfect as you."

He raised his eyebrows, a mischievous glint painted on his face. "I'm not perfect. In fact, right now I'm having very lascivious thoughts toward you."

She felt his body press against her own. All she wanted was for him to know how much she desired his love. Whereas the last few months she had been shy and even avoided eye contact, now she allowed her hands to pull against his strong back muscles in response to the sensation of him. Feeling him in such intimacy made her desire grow and she pressed her lips to his. Their mouths parted allowing their tongues to dance, their hearts to sing.

Daniel ran his hands down Raven's side, relishing the feel of her small waist, leading to the curve of her hips, which gave way to the roundness of her bottom. He squeezed her and she responded by rolling on top of him. Straddling him, she sat up and looked down at him with intention in her eyes. Slowly, she removed her top exposing a lacy bra that disappeared next.

His hands reached for her breasts and she threw her head back and closed her eyes, allowing herself to get lost in the moment, a time that she wanted to last and one she wanted to remember forever.

"This is perfect," she said, opening her eyes and returning to the moment.

"It gets better," he promised and as if to demonstrate this point, he moved his hand to deftly stroke the outside of her panties, lightly touching her and bringing her to want more.

"I think I might be overdressed for this party. Wouldn't you agree?"

"Indeed," he said. "It seems I am as well. Perhaps I should relieve you of these extra garments." He placed a finger underneath the waistband of her lingerie and with a light tug, indicated that he wanted to pull them off. She wriggled out of them, and in the brief moment that she moved away, he did the same and threw his clothes to the ground.

With the bedsheets askew they took a moment to admire each other's bodies before throwing themselves at each other, hands interwove into each other's hair, mouths moved passionately against lips and their chests pressed against each other. The intensity between them was heart-pounding and breathless, but Daniel was determined to show that this was something more. In a word, love.

It took a concerted effort, but he lightened his touch, gently running his hand over Raven's back in a soothing, soft tickle. One finger ran the length of her spine, bringing shivers to her very core. She gasped at the effect and as she did, his kiss moved just as gently over her lips, her jawbone, and across her neck.

"Oh my god," she whispered breathlessly. "You are magic."

He smiled inside, knowing that she had actually been with lovers capable of using real magic to bring a reaction. "This is something more powerful than magic," he said looking into her eyes, but not stopping his tender touch that moved between her breasts and down her stomach, and then daringly lower.

"It's love," she said simply and in return there was no need for elaborate sentences or gallant actions. He only responded with two words of his own.

"It's true."

Any remaining question about her feelings were answered. With their feelings matched, it was time they showed each other. He moved over her and she greeted him by parting her legs. He bent to kiss her and she felt his hardness against her. Wanting him, needing him, she pressed her hips upwards in greeting and he didn't need any more encouragement. Their dance began.

Arms and legs wrapped around each other, and hips moved in a slow waltz. Back and forth, slow and gentle with murmurs of love until their need demanded that their movement grow faster. With her legs squeezing his waist, she bucked her hips harder against him as he matched her intensity, pushing deep inside of her. From gentle lovers to athletes of endurance their lovemaking was choreographed to perfection, ending with both united in satisfaction.

# # #

Chapter Eleven

T hey slept. Daniel hadn't even realized he had drifted off until the light through the window reminded him of the day quickly departing.

"I better get to the crops," he said, sitting up and running a hand through his disheveled hair.

"So, you're making a break for it?"

"No! It's not like that. It could never be like that with you."

Raven smiled. "Relax. I know that. I'm just kidding you."

"Come here," he said pulling her into his arms again. They kissed as passionately after making love as they had in the precursor leading up to it. "I'm not going anywhere." After a beat, he added, "And to prove it, I'm really not going anywhere."

"You have to work," Raven chided.

"The crops can wait. It's just one day. What can happen?"

Together, they curled up and fell back asleep.

\# \# \#

Just like before, Daniel awoke first. He looked to Raven and mused about how beautiful she was. He had noticed her striking features last year, but now that he knew her through his own eyes and not those of her past enemies, he saw how misunderstood she had been and his desire to protect her brewed fiercely within him.

Ideas and images of an uprising still burdened his mind. He rolled over onto his stomach and rested his head on his forearm. Raven stirred and immediately rolled closer to him, her hands touched his back and he immediately relaxed to her touch.

As she gently massaged his tired shoulders she broached a subject that was long coming.

"How did you get here, Daniel?" It was such a simple question that Daniel was surprised it had never come up between them.

Without turning over because he loved the feel of her hands, he asked a question in return. He knew Raven must have spent many hours wondering about his circumstances, but it wasn't something one brought up.

"I'm not sure I can answer you completely, but even if I could, are you certain you want to know?"

The Romani Realms were not an easy place to survive and to do so meant living in the moment. Thinking about the past could be a suicide mission and she wouldn't dare unleash any more unhappiness unto Daniel. Yet, she could no longer ignore the possibility that he too could lose his soul in this place and she just couldn't bear to be here alone.

"I'm sure."

He rolled over to face her. "I don't remember everything," he said honestly. "Forgetting...that's the only good thing about this place. I do remember that I used to have sleepless nights filled with worry and dread, and even worse...guilt. I don't know what I did, but I do know it resulted in a death."

"It couldn't have been your fault," Raven said emphatically. "I know that about you. With all my heart and soul...what's left of it," she added with irony, "I know that you would never hurt an innocent."

Daniel nodded, wanting to believe her. "I remember a little girl. The sweetest girl you've ever seen. And, I know that I loved her. I'm told my crime had to do with retribution against someone who hurt her, but I don't remember the details. When I think about her eyes, her smile, it..." he swallowed hard and then stared out into the room that was growing dark with the coming of dusk. "I don't know for sure, Raven, but I think I killed a man who hurt this girl."

A chill ran through Raven's body, but she reached out to touch his arm. They sat in silence for a moment before she went on. "Daniel, if you wanted to remember, I would help you to do so, but some things are better left buried. Some memories are just too painful to relive."

She watched him carefully, wondering what was going on in his mind. She could have invaded his thoughts, made him think what she wanted, forced him to think only of her. But that wouldn't satisfy her. Theirs was a love she had never known. She and Phineas had been bound to each other and loved each other in their own way. In all truth, it was a strange way, sometimes like lovers, sometimes like siblings, but always born out of obligation.

Daniel, on the other hand, was human and wanted her. That was a powerful aphrodisiac. Never could she have imagined that someone would love her just as she was, but he did. He tore down her walls. He encouraged her to be truthful, and most importantly, he didn't begrudge her for the truth of her story. More than anything she wanted to give him her loyalty, but in the Romani Realms, survival could make that a fleeting circumstance, one that often remained just out of reach.

A nagging feeling gnawed at her heart. It was the feeling of dread perhaps born out of experience that nothing good had ever lasted for her. The fear of losing a grip on her current happiness made her uneasy. Although he had given her no reason to fear losing him, she fretted. She could easily employ her intuitive powers to read him and the future, but she reserved her demon gypsy powers for others, not Daniel. No, he was the one person that she would behave normally for. She craved the humanity that he brought out in her and she refused to give into temptation to live in an other worldly manner.

It was better to live in the moment and ignore the blistering thoughts that plagued her emotions. She felt so utterly safe with Daniel, so filled with unconditional love, that she couldn't bear to jeopardize it by reading him and certainly not by influencing him to behave in any way that he wouldn't do on his own.

"Daniel, I'm going to go for a walk."

"It'll be dark soon." His voice revealed his worry.

"I'll be fine," she reassured him. "I just want you to have time to think," she said as a way to give herself the same. "You think about what you want to do...what you want to remember, and then, when you're ready, you let me know."

He only nodded, not answering because he didn't have one to give.

# # #

Chapter Twelve

R aven needed answers. There were still a few
people who supported her position of power –
some of the guards, one judge, and maybe a small
handful of magistrates. The council as a whole may
have voted for her to step down, but she knew that
not everybody in the Romani Realms wanted her
gone. She couldn't rely on Daniel's protection forever
and it wasn't like her to cower behind a man. She
needed to regain her position and so she set out to
find her supporters even though it meant crossing the
woodland swamps.

She never liked this dark and damp area of the
Realms, but she proceeded nonetheless. She had
heard too many rumors and was unable to ignore the
same messages that worried Daniel. She needed to
separate panic from truth and stop postulating about
what ifs.

She walked through the area, avoiding the hands
that jutted up from the muddy ground, reaching for
someone...anyone...to hold onto. Raven jumped
lightly over each protruding arm, tisking at the dirty
hands that swiped at her ankles. She berated herself
for not wearing something more sensible. She should

have been in her jodhpurs and riding boots to protect herself from the mud and instead she left home still wearing a light sundress with heels that now sunk with each step. She hadn't wanted to change clothes or it would have aroused Daniel's suspicions. He would worry if he knew where she was going, but she couldn't hide under his protection forever.

Besides, it wasn't like her to rely on a man. She was used to calling the shots. She was an immortal demon gypsy for heaven's sake and Daniel, although quite capable, was still just human. She smiled at the thought of him. He impressed her and nobody had ever done that before. He wasn't afraid of this place and one should be. She was even fearful sometimes. Even though Raven had loved Phineas, she admitted to herself that the relationship was never born out of equality. She had the upper hand due to her position in the world and the fact that she had saved his life, extended it beyond that of his wildest dreams, and then taught him how to use his newfound powers. While he was intoxicatingly handsome and she loved him, she also wondered if she had not perhaps fallen in love with her creation of him – the man or rather, the demon gypsy, she had created within him.

Yet, demon or not, Phineas wouldn't have been able to be won over by Charlotte had he not possessed some humanity. Or maybe, his falling for her was just testament to what occurred every day in the Romani Realms...people attracted to innocent souls. To think that Phineas was just like the creatures at the other end of these hands, these dirty segments of limbs...Raven shuddered at the thought. But what really brought chills to the surface of her skin was the thought that maybe she was no better, which was why she was now attracted to Daniel.

She walked further and forced herself to contemplate whether it was possible that she could be using him for his innocence in order to give her peace so that she could carry on in this place. She shook her head against the idea. It wasn't possible. Her heart soared whenever she thought of Daniel. She didn't view him as she had Phineas, someone to oversee. For that matter, maybe Phineas had more free will than she knew. Thus far, the thoughts that she had sent to him were unanswered.

She had wondered if he would come to her rescue the way he had for Charlotte if things got too bad for her here. Realizing that she couldn't foresee that answer made her uneasy and all the more determined to protect herself and not rely on Daniel. She closed her eyes, forcing the wind to blow in the direction she must take. The sky darkened in response and the hands shrunk away so she could pass easily.

All she knew for sure was that she loved Daniel with a childlike purity. What's more, she believed that she deserved him and the happiness they had found. It wasn't his innocence that attracted her. He was too worldly wise in this Realm to even be referred to as an innocent. Certainly he possessed that quality because he wasn't corrupt like the council, but he wasn't naive either.

The very thing that Raven thought was his downfall – his goodness – was what won her over. He put aside everything that she had done to Samantha and still gave her refuge. He took her in when her home had been overtaken by rebel forces that were staging the uprising. The actual coup hadn't occurred yet and hopefully, it wouldn't, but Daniel had insisted it wasn't safe for Raven to be in the council quarters if she had been removed from office.

She looked upward at the fast darkening sky and increased her pace. There wasn't much time before the Buraqs and foot soldiers would be on patrol. It had been months since she had been back, but she had a small window of opportunity tonight. The crows were flying overhead and she could command the wind and its powers. She threw her head back, enjoying the feel of the gale force in her face. She owed it to Daniel to find out what possible atrocity she faced.

# # #

Chapter Thirteen

T he evening wind had picked up the way it always did in the evenings by the beach, but still Phineas looked up at the sky acknowledging that this was different. He and Charlotte walked along their quiet street following dinner. Again, he had been plagued by a headache so Charlotte suggested some fresh air might do him well.

As they walked, a murder of crows surrounded the corpse of a rabbit that had been run over. Charlotte carried on believing that Phineas was right behind her, but when she spoke and didn't receive an answer, she turned to find him observing the scene.

Turning back to him, she gave him a questioning glance.

"I keep getting messages from Raven," he explained. "I don't want you to worry."

Charlotte looked at him, but didn't respond. A million thoughts entered her mind at once, but each one sounded like the ramblings of a jealous girlfriend and since Phineas never gave her reason to doubt his commitment, she remained tight-lipped.

He still looked toward the birds and to her horror, she noticed that he licked his lips and his erection was noticeable.

"I never liked carrion. Raven made me try it once, but I was disgusted."

Something about Phineas' tone sounded as if he protested a bit too much. Charlotte had seen her friends' husbands insist that they didn't miss watching weekend sports now that they had babies to tend to and she heard the same regret in Phineas' tone as if he missed the shapeshifting that he had given up for her.

She knew this wasn't simply a matter of giving up a weekend hobby. Unlike football, no longer shapeshifting into a crow was removing a part of his nature. Turning off a switch that powered a necessary utility. She led him away from the carnage, but sucked in her breath when Phineas inadvertently turned to look over his shoulder just one last time. Even worse, he inhaled deeply and closed his eyes upon doing so and she knew that he was relishing a scent that ordinary humans couldn't decipher.

# # #

Charlotte put the key in the lock and had barely opened the door when Phineas pinned her shoulders to the wall and kissed her in a passionate embrace. Too surprised by his sudden interest, Charlotte couldn't move nor speak in reply. She kissed him back, happy for his renewed interest in her.

But his passion didn't dissipate into its normal tender loving. As if driven by the animal instincts they had just witnessed, Phineas pushed his body against Charlotte, letting his hands drift underneath her short skirt and pulling forcefully at her undergarments until they fell around her ankles.

He didn't even wait for her to step out of them before freeing himself from his own trousers.

"Phin, slow down," she whispered, trying to keep the sexy in her voice, but still wanting for him to behave more romantically.

"I can't help it." His answer was short, more of an excuse than a declaration of how passionate he felt toward her. His fingers entered her and when he discovered that she was not in the same frenzied state, he still didn't back off to kiss her more gently like he knew she preferred. He couldn't wait. He needed her now and so he dropped to his knees and spread her legs farther so that he could run his tongue over her.

"Phin please, why don't we go to the bedroom?"

She thought he heard her when he stood up, but he merely picked her up to carry her to the nearby couch where he once again crouched between her legs. He pushed his tongue inside her, holding her hands against her side. He kissed her with a driving force that didn't relent. When finally he tasted her response, he didn't waste a moment to change positions so that he could enter her.

"I need you." She couldn't tell if it was a declaration or an apology, but Phineas finished quickly, leaving his breathing erratic and Charlotte's heart uneasy.

# # #

Chapter Fourteen

R aven had planned to seek out one of the guards whom she knew still held an allegiance to her, but when she arrived at the building where council meetings were held she decided on a different tact. Although it was growing late, the Council was still in talks. This was highly unusual for a Sunday evening as Talia never missed an opportunity to watch the public feedings.

The feedings were the Romani Realms' own version of a pie-eating contest in which willing participants would feed upon the souls whose shelf life was just about to expire. There was a definite skill at hand. If one fed too long the nearly tainted soul would make the feeder sick to the point where they turned on themselves. If they didn't feed long enough, the very act of starting would drive them to such desire that they were likely to accept a soul that had absolutely no innocence left at all. The result of this action would be an overdose of low morality resulting in the loss of any remaining innocence in the feeder.

Talia never missed the feedings so Raven recognized that this council meeting must be of high importance. She snuck around the back of the building to where she happened to know that the guards would leave their posts in favor of a smoke while meetings were in order.

"They're coming back, you know. All of them." Myra's self-assured voice reached Raven's ears.

"Certainly not all at once. What do they think this is? A vacation destination spot?"

"Don't be silly, Talia. Samantha will get here first."

Howard began to hiccup. Raven instantly recalled the disgusting reaction he had whenever overly excited. "She's of pure soul! She is!"

"Calm down, Howard," Myra lamented. "She is and the one called Charlotte is as well. But remember, we aren't going to feed on them. They may be more valuable in other ways...such as recruitment."

"Well let's not let them get away this time," Talia complained, obviously annoyed to still be in talks. "Losing them was a tragic loss for the Realms. They were not only pure, but Raven had said Samantha had an unusual ability to tell if someone was innately good or bad. That means that her innocence extends deeper than the average soul. That is, if Raven's intel can be trusted."

"Do you think she's wrong?" Howard asked, beginning to sound as if someone had promised him a shiny new toy only to later inform him that the store was sold out.

"Don't worry, Howard. A soul like hers could be fed upon for years if we find the need. And the one called Charlotte is just as good. She will be coming afterwards."

For the first time since Raven had been listening, Talia sounded content to still be in the meeting. "You mean the White Dove? Coming here once again?"

Myra whispered conspiratorially. "She was one-third of The Triad. You know, three souls who together form an alliance that will control the secrets to the greatest minds the world has known. With those minds, they could harness enough strength, resolve, creativity and whatever else necessary to make the Realms bearable. We can even resemble the proper world and make it a haven that everyone would want to come to."

"Now you're talking," Talia said. "You see? It can be a destination spot. We can shroud the Realms in an appearance of what is most desirable to each individual causing them to willingly come here for a vacation, never to return back to their old life. Everyone in the Realms could just sit back and let the innocents flock."

"Yes!" Myra said with enthusiasm. "We can become another Las Vegas of debauchery and reap the rewards. All we have to do is get to Samantha before her friend Charlotte tries to bring her back and escape once again."

Raven held her breath, not believing the news. There was a time that she would have wanted to harness the power of the Triad with Phineas, but now she knew how power could corrupt and she wanted nothing to do with it. All she wanted was her quiet life with Daniel. Having Samantha and Charlotte come back here was the last thing Raven wanted. Innocents were needed in the Realms, but not those girls.

# # #

Raven left quickly, aware that she had stayed longer than was safe. Traveling through the marsh, she heard the foot soldiers but shifted into bird form to leave them far behind. Yet, when she arrived home she saw that they were just leaving Daniel's place. Again, she dodged out of sight, hiding amidst the corn field until she saw them leave down the long path back toward the forest.

"I'm sorry. You must have been worried," she said when she quietly snuck into the house via the side window.

"What are you doing?" Daniel was amused to see how agile she could be. "I would fly in through the chimney, but that would probably really freak you out. I just thought I'd be safe since they just left."

"Come here." He opened his arms to her and she readily moved into his embrace. "You know, it was too lonely and boring before you came to live here."

An awkward silence filled the room before Raven could decide how to respond. She knew that he probably wasn't lonely when Samantha was with him and she didn't know how to broach the subject that Samantha would be soon returning.

Raven decided to still live by her heart. It was her new motto and thus far, it had served her well. She stood on tippy toes and gave Daniel a kiss. "I want to do something for you. Something that you did for me when I first arrived here."

He furrowed his brow trying to figure out to what she referred. Unable to guess, he justs shrugged his shoulders.

"Go sit on the couch. I'll be right there." Raven left him to go to the bedroom where she retrieved a book, faded and worn, but still intact. Daniel had said it was his favorite. It was long and he had started reading it to her when she couldn't sleep at night, but that habit stopped when their conversation took over. Now she joined him on the couch and showed him the book.

"You're going to read me a bedtime story?" he asked amused.

"You did it for me. Now sit back and relax."

She started where he had left off and he smiled at the sound of her voice, especially when she laughed, which he realized wasn't often. "I love that sound," he interrupted.

"I guess I don't laugh enough."

"Nobody does here," he admitted. "There's little to enjoy. But I do enjoy your company. Very much."

They shared a look that was comfortable in the quiet. But a nagging thought wouldn't let her fully enjoy the moment.

Please, don't let my love for him be in vain. It's taken me lifetimes to learn to love – to trust in another and give myself to them. Please, don't take this away.

She said the silent prayer and then returned to the book.

# # #

Chapter Fifteen

J ames was only gone a day, but it was enough to make Suki miss him terribly. He returned to find Suki hosting a girls lunch out at the bar/restaurant. Charlotte cooed about how cute the couple was when Suki jumped from the table and dove at James with a running leap.

"Aww, look at that. They are so in love," she sighed.

"You and Suki are a constant reminder of my pitiful love life," Samantha lamented. "You know, I don't think I'll find a man to love because the only one that I do love is...away."

Suki returned to the table when James went to check on the kitchen staff. "So, what'd I miss?"

"Do Samantha's complaints about love count?"

Suki patted Samantha's hand like a doting aunt. "This will pass. You will find the one you're meant for."

"He's away," she repeated. "That's the word I use when I talk to people at school so they don't think I'm some sort of freak for never dating. I just pretend that he's in the trenches of war because he might as well be. That's what that place is like... a hell, a war that nobody will ever win and he'll be stuck there fighting against those sick creepoids forever."

"You could date," Charlotte suggested.

Samantha was quick to respond. "I don't want to. I want him and seeing you with Phineas and Suki with James..." her voice trailed. "I'm just a third wheel."

"You are not," Suki insisted. "I want us to be together forever, Samantha. I'm here until you and Charlotte use up your last wish and while you have the right to do that whenever it suits you, I will be sorry to say goodbye and I don't relish that day coming.

Charlotte spoke up for both she and Samantha. "We don't want that, Suki. We have no intention of ever using it. Do we, Sam?"

An awkward beat followed, but Samantha recovered her faux pas. "I'm sorry. I was just...thinking. Suki, as difficult as it is to see you make out with James, I don't want to be the cause of you leaving him either."

"I know it's hard, Samantha, but all those horrible cliches about love and loss have been spoken for years because they're true. You know the ones: time heals all wounds, it's better to have loved and lost then never have loved at all." Suki nodded enthusiastically, hoping the words would provide some comfort.

Instead, Samantha quipped, "Those were probably spoken by old, bitter women."

"Probably, but they do sound good at times like..."

But Suki never finished the thought. Her eyes went wide at the sight of James' reflection in the mirror. Only, it wasn't his true reflection, but rather a foreshadowing of him running in the Romani Realms. As soon as the vision struck, it seemed to fade, but when Suki caught James' eye, she knew that he had seen it too.

Something would cause them to return.

# # #

Chapter Sixteen

Phineas slumbered, but it wasn't peaceful. Throughout the night he thrashed at the sheets and groaned in what sounded like pain although he didn't wake. In contrast, Charlotte felt as if she didn't sleep at all. When morning came the sound of him in the bathroom awoke her, making her realize that she had finally drifted off, but daylight came much to soon.

Padding into the bathroom, she watched as Phineas shaved in front of his sink, wrapped just in a towel after showering. "Morning, are you okay?"

"Yeah, why do you ask?" he said, his voice muffled from pinching his mouth to one side in order to get a smooth shaving surface.

Charlotte stood with hands on her hips, wanting him to open up to her. She knew she wasn't imagining this change in him and certainly he couldn't feel rested after the night he endured. "You were moving about all night."

"I'm sorry. Did I keep you up?"

"Well that's putting it mildly, but I'm just as worried about you. It sounded like you were having horrible dreams." She reached for her toothbrush while turning on the water.

"I'm fine," he answered again, but the statement had just left his mouth when suddenly he gripped the sink, lowering his head at the same time.

Charlotte immediately turned off the water in her own sink and rushed to his side. "Phin? What is it?"

When he didn't answer, but placed his hand on his temple she pointed a finger at him.

"You see? Something is wrong."

Phineas opened the medicine cabinet and searched the bottles. "I'll be fine."

"Fine? And what are you doing now? You don't take medicine. You're immortal."

He located a bottle of aspirin, flipped the lid and popped two in his mouth, swallowing without ever taking a drink of water. "Well, I do now."

He crossed the room to Charlotte and gave her a kiss on the forehead. "Don't worry so much. You know what I do need?"

"What?" she asked, concern still laced on her voice.

"Coffee? You mind putting it on?"

Charlotte nodded and left the room. Phineas waited a minute to ensure she wasn't coming back before placing a hand on his abdomen and wincing in pain. He gingerly lowered the towel to inspect a dark, bluish bruise about the size of a walnut. He looked at it with concern, but wrapped the towel back up upon hearing Charlotte announce that breakfast was ready.

# # #

Chapter Seventeen

Throughout history, citizens turned to revolt as a means to protest a shortage of resources. The Romani Realms were no different. Angry over the disparity in the lifestyle between the elite and lower class, the soulless ones were threatening to go on strike.

The Romani Realms greatest commodity was innocent souls. But there were not enough to go around and the people were hungry. New souls periodically arrived, but most were immediately consumed with the government taking the best ones for themselves, leaving individuals with tainted morals for the rest. Immorality bred criminal behavior. The Realms was overrun with liars and cheats, rapists and thieves, not to mention the supernatural Buraqs that were used to keep the residents under control. But when not controlled, these creatures with the head of a horse and manly bodies, would pillage the villages whenever it pleased them.

Some residents were deemed worthy for their skills and left alone. Like Daniel, some could barter wares for their soul's safety. Others constructed objects of beauty, virtual mirages that pleased the arriving innocents and kept them from fleeing. But once the soulless ones moved into an area of beauty, the resources would begin to disappear at a rate faster than the builders could repair it. It was a dilemma that the government had yet to solve.

"A new boatload is arriving," Burl announced to the Council.

He looked over the balcony of the Realms' coliseum into the distant bay. Myra joined him. "Thank god. I'm sick of this last batch. So many vegetarians and do-gooders. You know," she said turning to Burl, "sometimes I find that one can be just too innocent. I like a bit of spice, don't you?" she said seductively, but received no response.

Burl just kept staring out at the distance, more interested in who was arriving than who was by his side. "Red heads are spicy," he said absently.

"No no no. She's off limits," Myra reminded.

Burl shrugged his shoulders as if he hadn't fully agreed to the proposition that had been made at the last Council meeting.

They watched as the captain escorted the boat load of passengers down the gangplank and onto a commuter bus. Just a short ride and they would be with them. Burl threw his drink back as if needing some artificial help to keep him from growing more impatient.

"Easy," Myra reminded. "You want a clear head when they arrive. The pretty ones aren't going to go home with someone who slurs his words."

"I'll be charming; don't worry."

Myra smiled. "You always are. So how long do you reckon you need?"

Burl pulled out a pair of binoculars and trained them on one girl dressed in a short mini skirt, a revealing halter top and high heels. She wore a bit too much makeup and laughed easily as she talked to the people around her. "I bet I can land that one after one drink."

"Excellent. I'll meet you at your place in an hour. See you lover."

Myra took off just as the new innocents arrived. She didn't have the patience for small talk like Burl, who looked at it like part of the hunt. Leaving him, she took one last glance over her shoulder as she saw him carrying two drinks and approaching the girl he spied. He smiled easily and she laughed at whatever he said before taking the drink he offered. Within one sip, the cocktail had its desired effect and she slipped into a zombie like trance before Burl led her out of the building.

# # #

Chapter Eighteen

T he bell tower rang in the highest mountain above the Romani Realms signaling to the residents that new arrivals had been prepared and would be available to those who could afford them. The price was to forgo visions of the Realms' beautiful landscape and live with the sight of its ugliness. In exchange for this reality check, the payee would receive an innocent that could sustain their mental well being.

Daniel and Raven heard the bell tower as it was located in the hills just above his cottage. They stopped their dinner conversation until its clanging ended, then sat one more moment in silence to acknowledge what would transpire.

"I hate hearing that thing," Raven said.

"Me too. Just be glad that we don't have to give into their rules."

Raven nodded. "I am, but sometimes I hate to think that we're on a level equal to Myra and the rest."

"We're not," he insisted. "They still feed. You and I...living in this place..." he said extending his arm to the farm that he cared for with such pride, "it keeps us pure of heart."

She took the last spoonful of the chocolate pudding Daniel had prepared and offered it to him. "You deserve the last mouthful. Because you are as sweet as this pudding."

He accepted the treat and smiled at her, reaching for her hand. "Thank you."

"For what?"

"For just being. Not asking, not making demands, and accepting that I'm a bit damaged."

Raven laughed. "You're the most normal damaged guy I've ever met."

"Any other guy would be all over you... all the time."

Her heart skipped a beat. "You're not like other guys. And that's a good thing. Don't feel like you have to give me anything. This is all I want."

He looked at his modest house with the Robin's egg blue curtains, cornflower yellow dishes still on the table, and then back at her. "I don't have much."

"It's enough," Raven replied and then, still worried about the possibility of Samantha's arrival, she asked, "How did you pass the time with Samantha?"

"You really want to know?"

"I want to know what makes you happy and I know she did. So yes, I guess I do want to know."

"We used to play Scrabble."

"Seriously?"

"Yeah. I'm really quite good at it. Made my own board a few years ago. Want to see?"

The relief Raven felt was obvious as she followed Daniel into the other room. "You are the epitome of what everyone here wants. You're able to take pleasure in the simple things. It's an innocent sweetness that you embody."

"You make it easy," he answered.

"You could use your crops for rationing, but you don't. You're not like the council members who are always trying to get more, take more. You're good."

"It's easy when I have everything I need right here."

They looked at each other with mutual appreciation, knowing they belonged.

# # #

Chapter Nineteen

D own deep, Suki was a country girl at heart. She had grown up taking long walks through tall grass, picking berries, and taking pleasure in nature's beauty. Living in the city had its own charms, especially for a girl with a serious shoe fetish, but there were times when she longed to get back to basics. Knowing that stress made this desire stronger, James surprised Suki with a picnic lunch catered by his restaurant and stole her away to an overlook on Mulholland Drive where they could catch sight of the ocean in one direction and the San Fernando Valley in the other.

It was a slice of quiet in the midst of the city where one could even hear birds chirping. Aside from the occasional Sunday driver, they were alone.

"Maybelline sent me home with your favorite, an entire sweet potato pie, as well as a surprise."

That news perked up Suki's ears. She pretended to sniff out the goods from where she sat.

"Uh uh," James shook his head. "I'm not dishing on the dish until you tell me what's put a frown on your pretty features."

"It's Samantha. I'm worried."

James took note of the way Suki tugged at her fingers when she spoke her thoughts. It was her own telltale sign that something was seriously amiss in her mind. "Would a pecan pie square help you tell me the rest?" He dug around in the picnic basket and produced a small tin foil wrapped package. The minute he opened it, the smell of molasses and brown sugar permeated the air and Suki thankfully accepted her slice.

He waited for her to take a few bites before pressing her for more details. "So..."

"She really misses Daniel."

"Yeah?"

"James, don't be such a guy. She was in love with him. And, she doesn't want anyone else. Ever."

"So she says. Suki, she'll get over him...because she has to. She can't pine for someone forever."

Suki raised her eyebrows as if challenging the statement. "You did."

"What do you mean?"

"You watched over me before I even knew. You must have fancied me to do so."

A worried expression crossed James' face, and Suki caught sight of it before he recovered.

"James? That's what you said. You did like me even before we met? Right?"

It wasn't like Suki to worry about the past. She had been around too long to focus on years gone by. But if the past with James wasn't as she believed it to be then wouldn't that affect her present and perhaps, her future?

He took her hand and lightly caresses the knuckles before bringing her hand up to his lips to kiss it. Even that gentleman like gesture sent shivers up Suki's arms for it reminded her of what he was capable of doing to her.

"You're pretty quiet," she noted.

"Suki, I did fancy you before we met, but the truth is that I wasn't exactly waiting for you. I had no idea how long it would be before you were in need of a Shade and so, I occupied myself."

"Raven."

The reality always came back to her.

James nodded and within seconds of his acknowledgment of the truth, Suki stood up to leave. "Don't go," he said and swiftly caught the same hand that he had just seconds earlier kissed. "It wasn't like it is with us. I mean, she was sick when I met her. I took care of her and then one thing just..."

"Led to another, I know."

"It wasn't a relationship; not like us. Please, Suki. Sit down."

When Suki did as he asked, James stared into her eyes, longer than he normally did as if he was trying to read the part of her mind that remained hidden. Finally, she relented to the gorgeous man who wouldn't turn away from her. Suki had gotten lost in James eyes before, which today appeared bluer than usual due to the sunshine that pooled down upon them. He leaned forward and kissed her lightly, before pulling her down onto the blanket and enveloping her fully.

When they separated Suki was breathless and James was forgiven. "Don't look so pleased with yourself. That was cheating," she mock complained.

"I'm your Shade. That means it's okay for me to read your thoughts. And they told me you wanted to be kissed. Long and good."

A blush spread across Suki's features and she leaned her head onto James shoulder where she stayed inhaling his scent and relishing the feel of his muscled chest. "I still don't know what to do about Samantha. You can't blame her for wanting something like this."

"Give her time. Things don't always materialize right away. Or disappear for that matter."

Suki suddenly pulled away, the same nagging thoughts accosting her. "Could you have had feelings for Raven after we were together?"

"Not romantically, but I did worry about her. She's damaged."

"That's putting it lightly."

James twirled a lock of Suki's long wavy hair between his fingers, wrapping the tendril around his index finger and then letting it fall freely into a curl. "What I meant was that she wasn't always the way you see her now."

Suki nodded, knowing better than anyone that he spoke the truth.

"Right. You know that. You used to be friends with her."

The phrase floated on the air. After all this time it was still hard for Suki to think about what was with Raven. Sometimes, losing a best friend was even harder than losing a boyfriend. As she thought about what Samantha was going through, James words reminded her of the loss she still felt for Raven.

"That was a long time ago," Suki admitted. "Her quest for power was stronger than everything else. She chose power over friends, lovers, family...and she always will. To believe otherwise is foolish."

James shrugged, not saying anything.

"How can you wear that expression? It's as if you're supporting her. Still, after all these years, James!"

"I just don't think she deserved to lose Phineas, even if he wants to be with Charlotte. He was all she had and now, she's...there. It must be horrible. Come on, Suki, you can't tell me you don't think about her? I know Phineas does."

With each statement from James' mouth, the shock on Suki's face grew incrementally. This last piece of news had her staring wide eyed and mouth open. "I know you're friends and you've got that man code thing, but you have to tell me what you meant by that? Is he unfaithful to Charlotte?"

"Of course not! He's here and Raven's there, but..."

"But?!" Suki said in disbelief.

"It's like you, Suki. You can pretend that you don't think about her, but we both know that isn't true. You still hurt over the loss of your friendship and as for Phineas, let's just say the history between them...well, that can't just disappear. They're connected."

"Okay so they share a past," she consented.

But James persevered with the hard truth that Suki didn't want to hear. "Not just a past, but also the present and future. It's like Maybelline and I," he explained. "One can't exist without the other. And there's more. The connection he shares to Raven...that occurs when a supernatural extends life to another person."

"Are you saying what I think you are?"

James looked at Suki gravely. "She gave life to Phineas and they are connected. But I also saved her, which means..."

"You too." She looked at him sadly, now realizing how fleeting love could be.

# # #

Chapter Twenty

Raven and Daniel had launched into a rousing game of Scrabble, but unlike any that she had ever participated in before. Like so many things in the Romani Realms, the ordinary took on new dimensions. In this game, every word played came with distinct intentions. Letters changed magically before their eyes to spell out desired words – words that initially were innocent enough, but gradually revealed Raven and Daniel's true feelings.

Daniel played the word "love" followed by Raven playing "true." Both smiled like school kids and continued passing the time of the long evening, each remembering what it was like before they found each other when time was a burden rather than something to be savored between them.

Earlier in the day Daniel had harvested wild berries and used them as delicious accents within his sugar cookies. He reached for one now, grazing Raven's hand with purposeful intention. She looked up at him questioningly, watching him enjoy the cookie of which he saved the last bite for her. He held the small morsel in front of her mouth and she readily accepted. As usual, a comfortable silence settled between them as they ate and played their game. There was no need for words other than those splayed across the game board.

After a bit, Daniel looked over wondering aloud, "When you were little what did you want to be when you grew up?"

"Why do you ask?"

"Why not? Is it something creepy like a serial killer?"

"No! Of course not. I wanted to be a veterinarian. I just wondered why you asked. Nobody ever has – well, I take that back. Suki knows."

"There's no telling how long we'll be holed up here together. I want to get to know you."

Raven looked down at her hands. She tore a strip off from her napkin and began twisting it into a ringlet. First one piece, then another until the napkin was littered in front of her.

"You're stressed out."

"No, I'm fine," she retorted, signs of the Raven he first observed evident. Her chin jutted out and she pushed her shoulders back in a proud stance.

"Yes, you are. You always do that," he noted her habit, "...when something bothers you."

"I've never met anyone who ever knew when something was bothering me. It's as if everyone thinks I'm an island, a cold, hardened woman who has no feelings."

"So what's bothering you?

"I found a picture of Samantha...a drawing actually. It was buried under some papers in one of the kitchen drawers. I know how hurt you must have been when she left. I guess I'm just feeling like I don't deserve your kindness."

Before Daniel could agree or refute the statement, a pounding at the door occurred. The foot soldiers had already made their nightly patrol and it wasn't like them to return. Caught off guard, Daniel and Raven looked to each other, panic in both their eyes.

Recovering from the surprise, Daniel hurried Raven along in their normal procedure. She moved swiftly to the main room and lifted up the rug to reveal two warped floor boards, which when raised revealed a crawl space underneath. Quietly, Raven slid underneath the floor, allowing Daniel to move the boards back into place, leaving her in darkness.

"Just a sec," he called toward the door, before messing up his hair and untucking his shirt to make it appear he had fallen asleep. When he opened the door, the foot soldiers came inside without invitation.

"Can I help you?" Daniel asked innocently, but the soldiers moved about freely, ignoring him. It was then that Daniel noticed that a corner of the rug that covered the hiding space was turned up. It didn't necessarily warrant suspicion, but it made Daniel nervous nonetheless.

He made a point of averting his eyes from the floor and waited. One trooper had entered the bedroom to perform a search and now returned, declaring the room clear. Satisfied that the house was empty, they moved to leave, but just before they reached the door, Daniel spied Raven's glass from earlier in the evening – a glass with lipstick around the brim. Discreetly, he grabbed the wine flute and held it behind his back...waiting.

"We're done here," the first foot soldier announced. "But we might come back." With that ominous statement and to exert his power, he gave Daniel a surprising shove against his chest, sending him flying backwards. Miraculously, he managed to maintain a hold on the glass as well as keep it hidden behind his back. Once they left Daniel waited until they disappeared down the path with their horses before retrieving Raven.

"I heard a scuffle," she said, her nerves evident.

"That was just me...having a torrid affair with the wall."

"Oh no. Are you hurt? Thank you...for everything." Her words weren't necessary as the appreciation was evident in her eyes.

"I'm fine and you're welcome."

"Do you think they'll be back?"

"Not tonight. But they won't stop looking for you. They need two things to survive here – innocent blood and power."

Daniel had forgotten how cold the basement could be until he noticed Raven shivering. "Here," he retrieved a throw from his couch and covered her shoulders with it.

"Again, your kindness presents itself at every opportunity."

"And what's wrong with that? You deserve it. By the way, that thing you said before we were so rudely interrupted...It's not true, you know," he added.

"How do you know? You still have her picture."

Daniel rose from his seat, which was across from Raven in order to move his chair right next to hers. He gently placed a strand of her black hair behind her ear and out of her eyes so he could look into them without the view being blocked. Lifting her chin, he made her meet his glance.

"Those eyes...," he didn't share everything in his mind, but it was clear what he meant. He was utterly captivated by her. "Dark pools of wonder. They try so hard not to show emotion, but I see what's behind them."

"Maybe you're misreading them," she answered, still obviously nervous that her own feelings wouldn't be returned.

"Raven, you don't have to be afraid of your feelings. You may have worked for centuries to bury them, but that only makes one more aware of their presence."

She shook her head and a tear dropped from one of those exquisite eyes, her lashes looking even darker from the escaped emotion. "There's one thing I still don't understand. It's the one thing we've never addressed."

"Just tell me."

"Daniel, why are you so nice to me? After...well, you know." She buried her face in her hands, pulling away from Daniel's touch and letting the tears flow freely.

He pulled her in close to his chest and let her cry against him. He rubbed her back, willing his soothing touch to relax and calm her. "It's okay...Raven, you didn't take Samantha away. She left on her own. Yes, I loved her. And you know what?"

Again, Raven shook her head, unable to form any words because her tears continued after hearing his admission.

"I wouldn't have met her if you hadn't sent her here."

"Lucky me," she said having finally recovered her voice. "I get to live with the knowledge that the only man that I have feelings for may still be in love with someone else. You kept her picture!" She swiped at her tears. "I didn't mean for that to come out. I'm sorry."

But then Daniel did something that surprised her. Taking her hands in his own, he pulled her off her chair and into his arms. Like that they remained. Nobody speaking, just holding each other. Until he finally admitted, "Raven, I lived here for years, maybe it was decades, I don't know because one tries not to count the days here, but regardless of how long it was, I had never experienced love because I wouldn't allow myself to. Samantha changed that in me, and just because she's gone, doesn't erase that need that now remains. I honestly didn't remember that the picture was there. I try to live in the moment. It's easier here to be that way. What I want now is to share my life again. With you."

Raven tentatively rested her head against Daniel's shoulder not only because it was there, strong and ready, but also because it felt so good to relax and trust in someone. "You are such a good person, Daniel. You can't let me take that goodness out of you and eventually I will. I'm like a cancer that attacks everyone near me. I can't help it."

"I don't want to hear that."

"You have to. Damn it, let me do one good thing in my life! Just listen to me!"

He kissed her fast and unexpectedly. And when she tried to fight him, by pushing against his broad chest, Daniel held her firmly as he was strong from years of working his land. His hands grabbed for Raven's wrists, pulling them to her sides as his kiss stayed steady on her lips. The intensity that he emitted finally reached her and she relented into him, her body relaxing without any fight left in her soul.

Daniel's hands released her own only to move up to her waist. Now holding her more tenderly, more assured that she wouldn't flee, his attention toward her was matched by reciprocation. She placed her hands on either side of his face and kissed him back while now laughing through her disappearing tears.

"The next time I kiss you, I don't want your salty tears ruining the moment," he declared.

"There's going to be a next time?" she asked incredulously.

It was Daniel's turn to release a hearty laugh. "Raven...you should know that there definitely will be a next time."

# # #

Chapter Twenty-One

S uki paced her apartment, trying to make sense of the turmoil of emotions that swirled in her brain. She loved James, that much she knew. She could even justify in her mind that he was a good man for helping Raven when he first met her. She knew that extreme situations could bring people close together and the fact that she was dying certainly qualified.

"I guess I can't fault him for taking care of her...and then falling for her," she mused out loud.

After all, it was hard not to be enthralled by Raven. She was vibrant and fun...well, when they were friends. Suki sat down on her couch with a cup of tea and remembered the way it once was with Raven. Back when they lived in London...before everything got so messed up.

# # #

"Does Pixie seem like she's not feeling well?" Raven bent down to pet her beloved dog.

"She seems fine." For a small dog, Suki was amazed at how quickly it walked as she struggled to keep pace with the dog and Raven.

"*I just don't think she's behaving like herself,*" *Raven continued.* "*Normally, she stops to water every plant we pass, but today it's as if our walk doesn't hold the same appeal it used to. I guess even for dogs, the same route in life can become mundane.*"

"*You're analyzing your dog?*" *Suki asked amused.*

"*Well, I always wanted to be a vet, maybe I could use my developing powers as an animal savant.*"

Suki leaned down to pat Pixie. "*Your mommy thinks she can communicate with animals. What do you think?*"

Pixie looked up to Raven and as pet and mistress made eye contact, Raven's eyes momentarily dilated and the dog rolled over on its back. Raven picked her up and announced, "*She's ready to go home now. I'm am too.*"

# # #

Suki couldn't deny that she missed their friendship. Of course, Charlotte and Samantha were akin to friends, but it was different. They were her Releasors. There was a boundary between them as well as the knowledge that they could cause her to be sent back to her bottle. With Raven, they were on equal footing.

Raven's powers developed faster, but Suki held her own and they shared a mutual respect. But when Suki expressed disapproval of the man Raven had been dating, their friendship suffered. Even when Raven was put on trial for witchcraft due to this man, the damage was done and Suki was never able to forge her way back. She never knew what happened to her after those times, nor had she discovered that Raven nearly died until James explained centuries later.

"I guess pride got in the way," she mused, thinking that she wouldn't let the same fault affect her. Even though Raven had been with James once didn't mean that Suki had to live in the past.

She looked out at the city lights from her penthouse window and wondered how she could have been so childish when a text from James pinged her phone. *I'm off in ten.*

James...a supernatural hottie. Who wouldn't fall for him?

"Don't go there," Suki chided herself, but her mind wouldn't behave and she imagined James with Raven. Logically, she knew that James wouldn't turn his back on a young woman, but did he have to then sleep with her when she was well?

She texted him back: *I'm sort of tired.*

James: *You sure? I could come up for a bit.*

Suki: *Do you mind if we catch up tomorrow? I'm really beat.* She loved him, but tonight she just couldn't allow herself to love him fully.

James: *Sleep tight. Love you.*

Suki: *I love you, too.*

She crossed the room and reached for her bottle, a beautiful cobalt blue with a butterfly emblazoned on the side. Holding it close to her heart she felt more at ease. This was home; it was comfortable. Yet, she didn't want to return to it. There would be no telling how long she might go without seeing James if she did so. And of course, being back in her bottle meant that one of her Releasors had used up their last wish, resulting in her return.

With that thought, a sudden vision struck Suki. Holding her bottle tightly, she recalled when Samantha was hit by a car and the black birds convened on her, biting and feasting on the blood that oozed from her injuries. She was sure that Raven had commanded the birds and quite possibly, she had shapeshifted so that she was among them.

The image was horrible and Suki was thankful to be jarred from the vision with the ringing of her phone.

It didn't take but a second to recognize Samantha's voice and hear the strain in it.

"What's wrong?"

"Suki, I'm sorry to call so late. It's just that I had the worst dream – a nightmare, really. It was when I had that accident."

"That's weird."

"Why?"

"I was just thinking about that time. My thoughts seemed like my own, though. It wasn't like when I feel your thoughts. When that happens, I see things from your point of view, but this was an imagery in my own head, more like a memory."

There was silence on the other end.

"Samantha? You there?"

"Yeah, I'm here. It's just that the same thing happened earlier between Charlotte and I. It's like I'm a conduit to both of you. Every one of my thoughts affects you two."

"Nonsense, we care about you. We're friends," Suki insisted, although the same nagging thought hit her again. They weren't true friends. As much as she loved spending time with the girls, they were brought together by the circumstance of Suki's imprisonment. Her freedom lasted only as long as her Releasors' ability to withhold asking for their third wish. "Samantha, people like us...it's normal to have a connection."

"Suki, I think it's more than that. It's like I feel this pull to the Romani Realms as if I have to go back."

"No! Samantha, you have to forget him. You're not going back." She had listened to Charlotte worry about this situation long enough. She would not pussy-foot around the subject the way Charlotte had. That was the role of Samantha's friend, but Suki was her advisor and her muse. She needed to hear the truth, no matter how difficult.

But the truth was only met by silence on the other end of the phone.

Finally, Samantha lowered her voice and replied. "That's not up to you, Suki."

Suki ignored the ominous tone in Samantha's voice. "Come over. We can talk. Watch a late night movie with me. I'll make hot cocoa."

"As you said, it's late. I'll see you tomorrow."

Suki held the receiver, listening in frustration as the line went dead.

# # #

Chapter Twenty-Two

P hineas hadn't flown in months. Captivity made him crave the freedom. As he swooped down low over the ocean, feeling the mist in his face, he realized just how much he had missed this...along with Raven. They came to land on the beach behind a sand dune that would have blocked the view of them even if it hadn't been night. And once returned to their human form, he rolled on top of her. Phineas didn't have any concerns weighing on his mind, his only thought was his desire and how to quell it.

Their bodies had memories and they fit together as if no time had passed. As Phineas entered her glorious body, he heard her call his name.

"Phineas!"

This time the voice was distracting and he woke to Charlotte shaking him.

"You were dreaming...and moaning. You woke me up."

"Sorry," he muttered.

Charlotte propped herself up on one elbow and admired his form lying next to her. "Well...seeing that we're awake now..."

"I need to get back to sleep."

"Later." Charlotte pressed against him and threw one of her legs over his form.

"Watch it." His tone held not a trace of romance, but rather, annoyance and even pain.

"What's wrong with you? It's not like I'm a linebacker."

Phineas lifted up his t-shirt to reveal the bruise that had now spread half way across his abdomen. "Oh my God, Phin. I'm sorry," Charlotte said, eyes wide. "How did that happen?"

Now, fully awake, he saw his dream as something entirely different...not a young man's fantasy, but a warning. He looked at Charlotte, shaking his head in wonder. "I don't know. I honestly don't know."

# # #

Chapter Twenty-Three

S uki was a long-practicing yogi having gotten into the practice of Hatha yoga at the encouragement of one of her past Releasors who was a devout Buddhist. She had often told Samantha and Charlotte that she came out of a session feeling relaxed and at peace, but on this particular day after taking Charlotte to a class, she admitted to not feeling any more zen than when she began the class.

"You look exhausted," Charlotte noted.

"I must say, you don't exactly look happy like a dead pig in the sunshine."

Charlotte crinkled her eyes at Suki, trying to ensure she understood the meaning of her phrase. She had learned that with Suki, the more distracted or worried she was, the more likely she was to utter one of her Southernisms.

"I didn't sleep well." Charlotte admitted.

"Me too. Samantha called me pretty late."

Charlotte looked at her in surprise. "She did? What was wrong?"

"Charlotte, I'm worried about her. She wants to go back."

"Back? Back where?"

Suki just raised one eyebrow, her right one, as that was the one that always proved to be more cooperative. She knew that Charlotte would get her meaning because she couldn't bring herself to verbalize the thought.

Finally, Charlotte said the words that Suki wouldn't...couldn't. "Not the Romani Realms. You can't be serious. Is she insane?"

"You tell me. You went on your own."

"That was different," she argued. "I was pissed at Phineas and I wanted to save Samantha."

"You could have used up a wish."

"I didn't want to lose you," Charlotte replied, shrugging her delicate shoulders.

"I almost lost you," Suki reminded her. "It would've been the same outcome."

"We can't let it happen again. We need to convince Samantha," Charlotte agreed.

"Something is pulling her there. It's as if every day her thoughts of the Realms grows more intense. I think there's something supernatural at play."

"What can it be?"

Suki sipped from her tea, but made a face. "Why can't yoga studios serve proper Southern sweet tea?"

"Because sugar is evil."

"Says the girl with the waif figure. Sugar is sweet. How can that be evil? Thankfully, James likes a bit of backside to hold onto."

"Speaking of James, might you ask him to help us?"

Suki didn't answer, but merely took another sip from her tea.

"Suki?"

"Things have been a bit strained. I don't know why. I mean, it's all on my part, but I don't know why I've been pulling back. Just a sense of something that I can't put my finger on."

Remembering the incident at her own house that morning, Charlotte pressed Suki. "What do you mean?"

Suki shook her head. "The subject of Raven has been coming up more than I care to admit. I don't know why. It's not like we used to talk about his past with her. He's thinking about her."

That admission made Charlotte worry. "Phin's been different too," she admitted. "I couldn't put my finger on it until you just brought up Raven. He's acting the way he did when they were together. A bit rougher around the edges. Seeming distracted and in need of a thrill. Our little quiet home life doesn't seem enough." She paused to stir her own cup of tea, before saying what else was on her mind. "I'm worried, Suki. I mean, how can I expect him to settle down with a baby? Maybe he's not the type."

Suki took Charlotte's hand in her own. "I don't know a man who is the marrying type. The kind who thinks to himself, 'Hey, I really want to have a baby.' But that doesn't mean they don't find their way to that place."

Charlotte sighed outwardly, trying to convince herself that Suki's words held a truth.

"It may not innately be in their genes, but eventually they all come around. Phin loves you. That's what you have to focus on."

"Maybe you need to take your own advice as well," Charlotte said wisely.

Suki nodded, but the look in her eyes said the task was easier said than done.

# # #

Chapter Twenty-Four

J ames walked up the path to his Georgian style home to find Maybelline already at the door. He thought to himself that she was a bit heavier than the last time he had seen her, noting that her white apron seemed to not fully cover the front of her pale blue dress. But keeping in the Southern tradition, James merely thought to himself that there was more of her to welcome and he extended his arms to her for a hug.

They wrapped their arms around each other and James felt the air go out of his lungs as Maybelline squeezed him hard.

"You are one strong woman," he gasped.

"Don't you forget it. Now, come on in here. You're just in time for dinner. Southern fried catfish and okra."

"No dessert?" he said in mock complaint.

"In time, in time," she said in her slow, syrupy accent that poured from deep within her throat. "Didn't expect you to be paying me a visit right now. All's well wheres you live? Suki a'right?"

James nodded, but remained tight-lipped.

"That's comforting."

"What?" he said annoyed that within five minutes of his arrival Maybelline was already wise to him.

"Even a man of few words like you, usually has somethin' kind to say about his girl, especially when that girl is quite out of the ordinary. Why she's prettier than a glob of butter melting on a stack of pancakes."

"That she is," James laughed. "But...something's just not right. She's distracted. I'm feeling twitchy. I don't know..." his voice trailed off.

"So you're a bit catawampus. It happens. Can you be more specific?"

James raised his eyes skyward, took a deep breath, and threw his head back. He stretched and rotated his neck in circles. "I honestly don't think I can until I get some food in me. It smells too good; it's damned distracting."

"Watch your tongue or you won't be gettin none." Maybelline flicked him with a dish towel and then led the way inside and toward the sunny kitchen. She bustled about, setting out dishes and checking the temperature of her frying pan. When the oil ran to the sides of the pan, she slid the catfish in, careful not to lose any of the egg batter or corn meal that coated it. The pan sizzled and she deftly adjusted the heat and shook it to and fro, cooking it evenly without breaking up the delicate pieces of fish.

Maybelline retrieved a platter from a sleek, silver warming drawer. Wearing oversized oven mitts, she placed the fish on the platter, dotted parsley around the edges because according to Maybelline, "There's nothing that dills my pickle like food that isn't presented well."

They took their places at the table and after James took a few healthy bites and visibly relaxed, Maybelline started in on him once more. "So what's troubling your mind, Mr. James?"

"Raven."

"That contemptuous wench? Why does she even have the privilege of occupying your thoughts?"

"I wish I knew. I was thinking you could tell me."

"Are you just thinking of her as in, 'Phew, I dodged a bullet when I cut that one loose?' or is it more along the lines of 'I miss that feisty mess and could give her a good one right now.'"

James put down his fork with a bang and looked up at Maybelline in surprise. "Never in all our years together have I heard you even come close to language unbecoming of a lady and here you are...talking like one of the men down at the corner liquor store."

Maybelline crossed her arms in front of her massive bosoms and sighed. "Well, I never thought I'd live to see the day that you'd go and get stupid on me."

"Maybelline!"

"Sorry!"

The two each took another bite of food, a tactic to diffuse the situation and bring back a form of pleasantry to the moment. Finally, it was James who spoke once more.

"But you're right."

And with that, Maybelline coughed up a storm until James gave her more than just a firm pat on the back. He whacked her straight between the shoulder blades.

"Thanks, I needed that. You surprised me."

"Thought I might," James admitted. "So, any reason why I'm thinking of her now? I mean, I'm happy with Suki. I want a future with her for as long as she'll have me. After all, as her Shade, I'm not going anywhere and having her as my girlfriend makes me feel less like a stalker. I hated those years when I was in the shadows. But now...now I just keep thinking of what it was like with Raven."

"And?"

"And? It wasn't even that special. She was sick, weak. It was purely for medicinal purposes."

"Uh huh," Maybelline looked unconvinced as she sat across from James with arms still crossed, shaking her head with contempt.

"I swear it." But after a moment, James relinquished the truth. "Well, it was a pity experience initially. But we didn't stop once she was healthy. I carried on and...yes, it was intense."

"While you were Suki's Shade?" Maybelline asked in disgust.

"Briefly," he admitted. "Very briefly. It was before I had the chance to follow or protect her. As soon as my assignment was solidified, so was my heart. I made sure to help Suki find her way, to ensure that her Releasors did right by her, and...that's when I broke things off with Raven."

"That explains things." Maybelline stood up to clear the dishes.

"Here, let me," James said, taking a plate from her hands. "You might throw it at me."

In spite of herself, Maybelline cracked a smile. James continued to clear the table while she moved to the counter to retrieve the pie. When they both returned to the kitchen table, appeased by the sight of the sweet potato pie with a gravy boat filled to the brim with whipping cream, Maybelline spoke the words that James dreaded.

"If you've been intimate with someone who lives in the Realms, your connection cannot be severed, and neither can theirs. It sounds to me as if Raven has found herself a new beau."

James pulled at his chin, wracking his brain for who would be crazy enough to get themselves involved with her. "Oh God," he finally declared. "Daniel."

Maybelline gave him a look as if to say, 'my work here is complete.' "I knew there had to be an explanation. You see, when Daniel, who was with Samantha, and Raven, who was with Phineas, get together...well, their partners living in the present get a sprinkling of their new found emotions."

"What about me? I'm not jealous."

"Of course not, you're a Shade. You're immune, but you are tuned into her...along with her past partners."

James looked baffled for a moment and then shuddered. "Oh gross. You mean, Phineas is thinking of her too? Right now?"

"Well, I don't mean right now, but yes...he's been with her, you've been with her. So you've got a bit of a connection to him as well. So, whatever no good deeds he's getting up to, you're feeling that energy."

James stopped eating and looked at Maybelline gravely. "Mayb...if Phineas and I were connected to Raven and we feel her energy due to her being interested in someone else, does that mean that someone who is interested in that someone else..."

"English, please!" she interrupted.

"Samantha! She's freaking out lately. I know she misses him, but it's more than that. She's desperate to return."

"She feels a pull to get back to him. Relationships in the Romani Realms can do that to people. At least now you know who she's been cozying up to."

"Ahh, shi__"

"James! You watch that mouth of yours."

"Yes ma'am."

# # #

Chapter Twenty-Five

Throngs of students dispersed for lunch and while Charlotte led the way to a shady table, Samantha started to fish through her sack lunch.

"Can't wait to get your hands on that scrumptious peanut butter and jelly," a girl with fashionable clothes cat-called.

Samantha rolled her eyes and stuck her tongue out at the girl. "New school, but same old cliques."

"We couldn't exactly go back to our old school."

Samantha sat down at the table and dug into her lunch. "No, reincarnation has a tendency to freak people out."

Charlotte smiled and held up her own sandwich in a toast. "It's only one semester. We'll be out of here and released into the big wide world in no time. I can't wait. I am so over high school."

Samantha polished off the rest of her sandwich and looked at Charlotte, who took demure bites in her typical fashion. "What are you going to do?"

"What do you mean?" Charlotte looked up at her friend. "About?"

"We may have only missed a few months here, but we sure messed up our lives."

Charlotte looked down at her sandwich, not wanting to agree or disagree with her friend. Finally, she went for diplomacy. "I'm sure things will work out. They have a tendency to do that."

Samantha nodded, but seemed unconvinced. "You wanted to be a doctor, remember? Have you even applied to colleges?"

"No, but...I can take a gap year. There's always time to go back."

"It's because of Phineas. You have someone here that satisfies you. You don't feel a need to leave and do something."

"Maybe," Charlotte agreed.

"So why can't you understand that I want the same?" Samantha's voice rose with her passion.

"Is this what you're really talking about? Going back to the Romani Realms...for Daniel? Samantha, I may be putting off college because of Phineas, but it's not just a simple high school crush. We're going to have a child together. I've seen the future and I'll have to figure out college when the time is right."

"And the time will be right when you have a baby?" Samantha asked, sarcasm dripping from her voice.

Charlotte didn't answer.

"I'm sorry," Samantha finally spoke. "We never used to fight."

"No, no we didn't." Charlotte met Samantha's gaze. "I'm trying to understand, really I am, Samantha. You have a point about my future, but then again, I'm not exactly like other high school girls, am I?

"There's a number of reasons why I can't just pretend that I'm living a normal life. Phineas has wealth from decades of savings. That will give us stability. I want to work, don't get me wrong, but I don't need to right now and more important to me is being reunited with Shadow, whom I love."

"That's all I want! I love Daniel; don't you see the similarity?"

"A love for a child is not the same as a love for a partner."

The two girls were at a standstill. Each sat with arms crossed, their body language showing their frustration with the other.

Charlotte picked at the remains of her sandwich, throwing the crust down to a pigeon only to have a large raven swoop down and get it first.

"I can never look at those birds in the same way. I always wonder if they're one of them," Charlotte said, shooing the bird away with her feet.

Samantha nodded. "How did you do it?" She asked quietly.

Charlotte immediately knew what she was referring to. "There were so many forces at work. Everything just came together at the same time. I was meant to go back–in order to bring you back."

"You can't tell me?"

"Samantha–I'm not trying to be coy. I don't really know how I returned to the Romani Realms. I had a deep desire to find you. Phineas had betrayed me...at least I thought so. Raven wanted me to go there. So, with my desire and her powers...I guess it all just fit into place."

Samantha nodded and wiped away a tear that slid down her cheek. Charlotte crossed to the other side of the table and took a seat next to Samantha. Leaning her head in closer, she offered what comfort she could, hoping to remove the pain that plagued her friend.

"Love is powerful. Love never ends," Charlotte said as a way of showing her understanding.

Samantha met her friend's gaze. "You are my best friend. What you did for me was so unselfish. I don't mean to not be grateful to you, but I can't live like this. Something just pulls at me to go back. Please don't hate me for feeling this way."

Charlotte smiled and shook her head, a peace coming over her. She admired her friend's honesty. It was the trait that gave Samantha her gift...the ability to sense a person's true nature. And in turn, Charlotte was gifted with a didactic memory, the ability to remember every fact ever learned. It made her wise beyond her years and with that knowledge, she realized that there was no point in fighting this argument.

"Samantha, I could never hate you. You don't owe me your life. It's yours to live."

Samantha crumbled up the paper bag that had contained her lunch. She aimed at a trash can a few feet away and easily made the basket. A small and meaningless victory, but one that signified more to come, at least in her mind. For the first time in weeks, a smile broke out on her face and Charlotte took note of it.

"I want you to hear something," Charlotte spoke slowly, stressing the importance of what she was about to say. "Love is patient and kind; love does not envy or boast; it is not arrogant or rude. It does not insist on its own way; it is not irritable or resentful; it does not rejoice at wrongdoing, but rejoices with the truth. Love bears all things, believes all things, hopes all things, endures all things. Love never ends. Corinthians 13:4-8."

"Love never ends," Samantha repeated.

Charlotte took her hand. "You've made your choice. I'll help you."

# # #

Chapter Twenty-Six

The Buraqs, creatures with muscular bodies depicting the strongest of man but with heads of horses, patrolled the Romani Realms on orders of the high council. They were treated like animals by the rulers, slave labor, in fact. As such, they were afforded no clothing, not even a loin cloth to cover their bodies. And, like animals they behaved.

They were accustomed to taking what they wanted if given a chance. When their superiors weren't looking or chose to look the other way, the Buraqs would steal food from homes, rape women, and deposit their feces whenever and wherever the impulse hit. Because they weren't given any privileges, the rulers of the Romani Realms determined that these "small concessions" as they referred to these offenses, were an even exchange for the Buraqs' pliable loyalty.

Loyalty could be bought. Escaping servitude could be accomplished for a bribe. However, it was rare that someone facing this fate was in the position to bribe an official. Raven, once among those who sat at the top of the food chain, now found herself on the outside and facing the fact that the Buraqs, who ironically were bred and trained to do her bidding, were now the same force who hunted her like a fox for sport. Their loyalty was fleeting and had been bought by those who had even less humanity than Raven – those who never had even a grain of emotional conscience within them.

Those were the ones who stood on the edge of the woods, cheering on the Buraqs in their quest to bring back Raven and anyone else who had once served on her cabinet – now referred to as infidels. It wasn't easy to take power away from Raven and her disciples, but she had been distracted by her quest of the Triad. Her choice to chase after Samantha and Charlotte had resulted in a perfect storm of sorts, providing an opening for those jealous of her power to steal it away.

"Weak! That's what I was," she muttered to herself. "I should have kept my eye on the ball." Raven shook her head to herself, knowing that she wouldn't have been any better off had she maintained her focus on controlling the Romani Realms. It was anything but an ideal place to live. Heck, she didn't even like visiting, but it was a necessary practice to maintain the control she needed in the present world. When she had power, individuals stuck between two planes – in the Romani Realms and the present world – were able to be borrowed and transported as she needed reinforcements.

"And for what? Why did I even care?"

It was the first time Raven even dared let the thought enter her mind. To consider that a lifelong quest was pointless and futile only served to shine a light on one's own actions and considering that Raven had over three centuries under her belt, the idea that her time had not been well spent wasn't something she enjoyed entertaining.

"Trouble is that I'd rather cut off my own arm than spend time with these...animals," she said aloud with distaste, her thoughts going to the reason why she stayed away for so long. "Humans aren't so foolish after all. Get married. Settle down in the country. Have kids..." She chuckled at the thought of herself living such a suburban existence.

"Phineas would have certainly gone for it," she huffed as she plowed onward, not knowing exactly where she was headed, just knowing that she needed to get away from the immediate threat. She kicked at the dirt as she went, chiding herself for being so foolish as to take another excursion alone and away from the safety of Daniel's cottage. She silently vowed to one day be happy with where she was in life.

"If I'm going to take a lesson from the human handbook, I might as well say that we just weren't meant to be," she mused, thinking back to Phineas and wondering why he had entered her mind at all.

Still, the thought of domesticity calmed her and allowed her to focus on her senses – traits of that were normally of superior strength – sight better than any bird of prey and hearing keener than animals considered to hold the record such as dolphins, owls, and bats. But in the Romani Realms her senses were impaired to being only twice as strong of average humans, rather than ten times, which was the norm for her.

"Ahead!" a deep voice with a gravely, inhuman tone sounded in her ears. The Buraq must have been nearly a mile away, but Raven's hearing picked up his conversation.

"She's the last one of the old council that needs to be rounded up. The others have been brought in already."

Raven gave a momentary thought to her comrades, but shook off any feeling of sympathy knowing that they didn't have any human emotion left in them and as such wouldn't feel fear, which she knew to be a far worse circumstance than the resulting death. As for herself, she now realized how much of Phineas' former humanity had rubbed off on her. As much as she had tried to rid him of emotion, she knew it was what made him susceptible to Charlotte's charms. And maybe, just possibly, it would end up saving her as well.

As she ran through the woods, the only thing that kept her a few paces ahead of the creatures who would certainly rape and beat her if they caught her, was the fact that she knew how they thought because she had programmed them. Their needs were simple: food and sexual satisfaction. As long as she kept one need fulfilled, they could be distracted from a mission. Raven couldn't stay in bird form long in the Romani Realms where the air was thin and made her transformation exhausting, but she could switch long enough to use her keen eyesight and her own hunting skills to her advantage.

Flying stealth-like, she spotted a burrow and waited above the treetops for the rabbits to appear. She dove and killed them off one by one and then transformed back into her human form, gathering the rodents up in her cape that she now used as a knapsack and throwing one into the trail behind her for the Buraqs to feast upon. When her strength returned, she would transform once again, locate more rabbits and carry them by her sharp talons. Systematically, she would drop the dead rodents where the Buraqs would find them, driving them off her course.

The process was slow and tiring, but it gave her a far enough lead that she might just have a chance at surviving the night.

# # #

Chapter Twenty-Seven

Although still seemingly distracted, Phineas lounged on the couch with his head in Charlotte's lap. The television show they watched grew more intense and although the action on the screen would be of interest to most, Charlotte couldn't help but focus on the bruise that displayed on Phineas' abdomen as he shifted ever so slightly. It was growing in size and its color became darker.

Running her hand through Phineas' hair, she was pleased when the show ended and she could broach the subject on her mind.

"Phin? How did you develop your powers?"

"Did that show give you ideas? Being supernatural is typically reserved for Hollywood, you know."

"Silly. I'm just interested..."

He propped himself up to look at her. "Well, it's not something that comes from a T.V. script. For that matter, you can't read a book and research it, Miss Supernatural Brainiac."

She kissed his forehead, smiling at the new nickname. "Yes, but surely you must remember what it was like before...before you were like this." She jerked her head toward his stomach, indicating the bruise.

"Is that what this is about? I'm fine. It doesn't even hurt."

"That's even more reason to be concerned. It's not normal," she emphasized the last word.

He took her in his arms, changing positions with her. "Normalcy is overrated. But, since you're so interested, I'll tell you. When I died and was brought back by Raven, I got a boost in everything – sight, sound, smell, perceptions."

Charlotte asked, "Emotions too?"

"In the sense that I can tune into someone else's," he said pointedly. "Is there something else that you're not telling me? Charlotte, what's this all about?"

She took a deep breath and exhaled, finding the strength to reveal everything. "It's about Samantha. She's an adult. She can make her own decisions."

"Eighteen is technically an adult, but one is hardly able to make life changing decisions at that age. At least, one shouldn't make them. An eighteen-year-old girl can change her mind as fast as she changes her wardrobe."

Charlotte smiled at the analogy. "You're right, but she's determined. Raven helped me get there before. I need your help this time."

"You're not going there," Phineas raised his voice.

"No, not me. Samantha."

"Oh that's just great. Now I'm going to look like the ass again. How can I say that it's not okay for you to go there, but it is for Samantha?"

Charlotte shrugged. "I'm not asking for your opinion. I'm not even asking for the knowledge of how she gets there. That, I already know." Charlotte began rattling off a list of applicable facts. "Time and space continuum, the theory of compossibility, quantum entanglement...you know, the usual."

"Show off," Phineas said, but his admiration for her memory was obvious. "So if you know all this, what do you need from me?"

"What I need is that boost you were speaking of. Raven propelled me into another realm with the black magic learned from being a demon gypsy. Samantha needs the same."

"She may not come back."

"I know," Charlotte replied. "But living here without Daniel...that's not living at all. Her heart is already there."

# # #

Chapter Twenty-Eight

S uki waited at the bar for James' return and upon seeing him, ran into his arms. When she pulled away, she noticed a small spot of sweet potato on his cheek and dabbed at it with her finger. "You did bring me back a slice?"

"Of course. I wouldn't live it down had I forgotten," he said retrieving a slice from his backpack.

As Suki eagerly accepted the offering, she asked, "Did you learn anything interesting? Because the girls' seem more distant than ever." She paused momentarily as if in thought, but then continued. "Who knows...maybe it's just teenage angst, but it's not like them. Has Phineas said anything?"

James seemed hesitant to admit what he learned, especially since it partly involved his past with Raven, but Suki had an instinct where that woman was concerned and could tell that he was holding out on her.

"Spill it, James."

"Alright, but promise me that you won't overreact."

Suki put her hands on her hips. "Now that's a great way to start a conversation with a woman."

Having been aptly chastised, James smiled slyly and began what he had to tell her. "So, you know that where you and I are concerned, our past connections can still create a draw to others...others who are supernatural."

"Yes, but Samantha is human. I can understand, although I don't like it, that you can feel Raven – gosh even saying that grosses me out – and I get that the same applies to Phineas – gosh that's like some kind of wrong threesome," Suki closed her eyes and shook her head as if trying to clear her mind of the imagery.

James moved to hold her in his arms. "I know, don't say it."

"Fine. Moving on...it doesn't explain why Samantha can't just get on with her life."

"Except that she really loves him. I know that I don't even want to fathom not being with you – now that we are together," James said, his eyes smiling down at her. "I watched over you for decades, wanting to be with you, but not able to be near."

"But our love is different."

"How so?"

Suki thought for a moment, searching for the right words. "Love is powerful. And first love maybe even more so, but that place...that's not the kind of place you go back to – love or not – unless something is pulling you. What can it be?"

James nodded his head, knowing Suki had hit upon an accurate point.

"Maybelline thinks the soulless ones might be orchestrating it."

"Why? How?!"

"They need fresh innocents to feed on."

Suki paled. "But Samantha is just one person. How did they even think of her when she's not even there. Why her?"

"Listen to me," James took her hand in his own. "It won't be just her. Just like she is pulled toward Daniel, we already saw how she and Charlotte have a connection to each other. Growing up without parents, they have a very strong bond."

"So if Samantha goes back, Charlotte will follow?" Suki pondered her own words, but quickly backtracked, "No, I don't believe that. She's happy here...with Phineas, even though I hate to admit that her future is tied to a demon gypsy."

"Oh, she'll be with him – he'll end up there too."

"No. James, tell me that what you're saying isn't definite."

But he couldn't utter the words she wanted to hear. "There's no escaping it. The only thing we can do is keep Samantha out of there...for all our sakes."

"But from what you say, she'll spend a lifetime in misery."

"One life. Or three? Maybe yours and then mine as well."

"The greater good?"

"Sadly, it's true."

# # #

Chapter Twenty-Nine

R aven had been running throughout the night with her stress level increasing as quickly as her energy decreased. The woods were treacherous with muddy pits that threatened to consume one if you stumbled within them accidentally. Keeping to the edge of the woods was the safest path, although also the longest. Hours of slow movement had resulted in Raven becoming turned around, not realizing that she had reached the end of the Romani Realms border, which was both a blessing in that it was far from where the council resided, but also left her trapped with little in the way of an alternate path should the Buraqs find her.

Looking around, she saw a grove of trees and flew toward them, a place to take refuge for a few hours. As she sat among the branches, cold and huddled under the shroud of darkness. She knew Daniel would be worried, but she was too tired to carry on and it was just too dangerous. She allowed her eyes to close as she fell asleep remembering that her situation was very similar the night she came to Daniel for the first time.

#

On the run, she spied Daniel's cottage at the end of a path surrounded by the cornfields and vegetables that he carefully tended. Like everything in the Romani Realms, Daniel's property was another example of contrasts, a slice of peacefulness on the outskirts of a war torn land, his vast fields and groves of citrus trees were a welcome invitation to her travel weary body.

Raven transformed into bird form and took refuge in one of the trees, staring over the property and letting her eyes rest on the patio table that still had the checkered cloth she remembered from six months earlier. She had barged into a domestic scene if ever there was one. A dinner party among friends, couples paired up like Noah's arc: Suki and James, Samantha and Daniel, and Charlotte...cozied up to her Phineas as if they had been meant to be.

"Well, perhaps they were meant to be," she had said to herself, transforming back into human form despite her wish to remain a bird. She was tired and weak, unable to fully control her own powers. Even worse was the presence of a tear forming in her eye. "Damn!" she shouted aloud, angry that such human emotions were plaguing her.

Her shouts caused a light to go on in the tiny cottage and no sooner, the front door opened. "Great," she muttered to herself, shifting quickly into bird form, the effort of which caused her to nearly drop from the branch where she perched.

A flashlight's glow passed down the walkway, illuminating the path leading up to the front door.

When still she didn't move, Raven thought she had gone undetected, but no sooner had the thought come that it became a distant one as Daniel then shone the light directly onto the tree branch where she unsuccessfully had tried to blend in with other crows.

"You can't stay like that all night. The nights get cold in this part of the valley."

Still in bird form she stared at him. It wasn't possible for him to recognize her.

"Yes, I'm talking to you, Raven," Daniel had said. "Do you want to come inside? That tree has very little foliage to protect you from the night air...or intruding eyes."

She was slightly larger than average crows, but other than that, there was no way for a human to detect her in shapeshifter form. How did he always seem to be a step ahead of everyone else?

"Raven, I'm getting cold so if you don't come in here now, I'm going to leave you and go inside to finish the bowl of popcorn I just popped."

Perhaps it was the fact that she had shifted so many times in this one day, but the thought of kernels was too tempting to turn down. She glided down from the branch, landing directly onto Daniel's porch where she transformed and rose before him draped in a black gown with bell-shaped sleeves that mimicked the look of the wings that she no longer bore.

"Now that's an entrance," he said and turned to go back into the house. Baffled by his lack of fear or surprise of her presence, she stood there momentarily dumbfounded. "You comin'?" he called over his shoulder, his eyes holding an amused

expression for the stubborn Raven who was now a
reluctant house guest.

# # #

Raven slept, although not soundly. The wind blew
through the tree and periodically she would awake
with a start, only to reluctantly remember that she
had to remain outdoors for the night. She folded her
wings around herself hoping that sleep would follow.

# # #

Chapter Thirty

"Y ou're sure about this?" Phineas asked, holding Charlotte's hand while gently rubbing his thumb over the back of it. The rhythmic motion calmed her and she turned to Samantha, her eyes silently asking her friend the same question.

"It's what I want," Samantha responded, kicking up the dirt around her, and staring uneasily at the headstone that once marked her own grave.

Phineas glanced at Charlotte once more to which she simply nodded once in response.

"Okay then. Sit down." He pointed to an old, wooden table that had been discarded in the corner of the old cemetery. Probably at one time flowers had been placed on it during funeral proceedings, but now it was just another ancient castaway in the forgotten graveyard.

Phineas motioned that they should sit around the table, and Charlotte and Samantha did so hesitantly. The table had a single hole in the middle where a sun umbrella would have once stood. Instead, a white rabbit was placed over the hole, positioned so the single, but deep cut that stretched across the underside of its neck dripped its blood in a slow, steady stream to a waiting bowl that sat on the ground.

Charlotte and Samantha looked at the rabbit with disgust, but sat down opposite each other nonetheless. With a piece of charcoal in his hand, Phineas began to draw the points of a pentagram, connecting one angle to Charlotte, the next to Samantha, and extending one more to the chair that he would take, and finally, the two remaining points to two empty seats.

"Are we expecting James and Suki?" Samantha asked.

"Suki wouldn't..." Charlotte started.

"No, she would be furious if she knew I agreed to this. And James, he'd have my hide."

Charlotte pointed to the extra seats that made up the final points of the pentagram. "Then what are they for?"

"Life...and Death." Phineas looked to the girls, "Are you ready?"

# # #

"Try this one," James said, placing a drink in front of Suki.

She accepted the tall, thin glass that was already sweating from the unseasonal heat outside in contrast to the ice cubes that floated inside along with slices of pineapple that mixed with the amber liquid. Stirring it once with a straw, a small pout crossed her features.

"What? You haven't even tried it yet."

"I'm just wondering when pineapple became an ingredient in a traditional mint julep."

"I never said it was traditional; it's exceptional. Trust me." James crossed his arms in front of his chest, his short-sleeved shirt now giving Suki a view of his well-defined biceps.

"Bourbon or rum?"

"Bourbon. Taste it."

Suki placed the straw between her lips and took a delicate sip. Her eyes widened with delight and she immediately took one more.

"I am vindicated. Told you."

"Never would I have believed that you could top what I became accustomed to in New Orleans, but this...wow James, this is..."

"Exceptional?"

"Exceptional," she agreed. "Have one with me?"

He brought over a pitcher that contained more of the cocktail and poured himself one. "Seeing that we're now closed, I'll join you. You want to know the secret?"

"You're willing to share your secrets with me?" she asked coquettishly.

"I am. Every last one of them."

A cold wind blew in from an open window as it often did when Suki's memory brought up anything unpleasant. James quickly placed a hand over a stack of cocktail napkins that sat on the bar before they blew out of place. "Suki?"

"Sorry. I'll just..." she rotated her hand toward the window and the breeze immediately died down.

"What was that about?"

"If you must know, when I heard you mention the word 'secrets' my mind went to that zinger of a secret I discovered about you and Raven."

"Powdered sugar," he said changing the subject.

She sent him a baffled expression. "Is that some sort of new Southern term of endearment?"

"No, Sugar," he drawled in imitation of Suki's typical phrasing. "It's my way of getting us off an unpleasant topic and onto one of more interest. I use powdered sugar instead of cane sugar in my mint julep. It dissolves better and has a thickness that combines with the bourbon to create a superior drink. And, I muddle the mint."

"You what now?"

James demonstrated by placing a sprig of mint leaves into a small bowl that resembled a pharmacist's mortar. Then, using a device like a piston, he careful began to compress the leaves. He added them into the drink before taking one last leaf between his thumb and index finger and rubbing them together. Holding his hand up to Suki, she bent her head and inhaled the fresh scent.

"It's like a bit of home," she replied, closing her eyes and relishing the way a simple sensory memory can bring another back. "I feel better already."

He stepped behind Suki and placed his hands on her shoulders. He gently started to massage her neck, instinctively moving his hands to exactly where any tension remained and pulled it from her. "Maebeline first showed me to muddle the leaves, or as she would say, 'massage the mint' before adding the liquid. It gives a more full-bodied effect rather than just floating a few leaves on top."

He moved in front of her, allowing his hands to run down her spine as he pulled her in close to him. Feeling his strong chest against her own, combined with the effects of the alcohol made Suki feel positively light-headed. "Strong-bodied, indeed," she whispered, tilting her head upwards.

James didn't need a better invitation. He dipped his head toward hers and their eyes met. There was nothing either of them wanted more than to connect their lips and feel the warmth of each other.

Each moved slowly toward the other until their mouths were just inches apart, coming closer to fueling their desire. Their kiss was imminent until a sudden flash of electricity followed by the crack of lightening and an eerie chill in the air became far more perceptible and ominous than the wind that Suki had earlier conjured. The cold air made James instinctively wrap his arms even tighter around Suki, both of them immediately knowing that something supernatural was at play.

# # #

Chapter Thirty-One

In spite of it being mid-afternoon, the sky grew oddly dark with a sudden influx of clouds moving overhead. Wind and rain pounded the ground, but did nothing to offset the constant drip sound emanating from the draining blood of the rabbit that lay in the center of the table.

As if a bull horn was amplifying the sound, Charlotte and Samantha could do little to ward off the horrific noise from their ears. Phineas' eyes were closed, his head nodding forward and back in time to the drip drip drip.

And when the blood had all but drained, leaving the rabbit thin and merely a fur shell to its former self, Phineas opened his eyes to reveal only blackness.

"Phineas?!"

"Charlotte, don't. Look!"

Samantha pointed to the center of the table where the rabbit was now levitating above the glass surface. As it rose, sparks flew from it. The sky continued to darken, clouds moving faster in time with the increasing wind.

"Je pense, donc je suis...Cogito ergo sum..."

Samantha looked to Charlotte, who with her didactic memory, the ability to recount anything ever learned, would most likely have an idea of what Phineas was speaking of. "Any clue what he's talking about?"

"It's a phrase spoken by René Descartes, first in French and then once more in Latin. It means, 'I think, therefore I am.'"

"What does that have to do with transporting me to the Romani Realms?" Samantha wondered aloud.

Phineas, still in a trance, spoke again. "Mysterium fidei." He repeated each of the phrases continually, his head nodding, his eyes still unseeing and black.

"He's recounting the foundation for all knowledge," Charlotte said, her forehead pinched in deep thought. "That, and the next phrase, simply translated to: 'the mystery of faith'.

"The mystery of faith..." Samantha repeated.

"That's it!" Charlotte exclaimed. "Samantha, we must recount everything we know about the Romani Realms...how you got there the first time...when..."

Charlotte couldn't bring herself to finish the thought, but Samantha did so for her. "You mean, when I died?"

Charlotte nodded. "Yes, and the same is true for me...when I went to find you there. Take my hand and concentrate."

"Charlotte wait," Samantha pulled back her hand. "I don't want this to affect you. What if you are sent back as well?"

"It won't happen. I trust Phineas to keep me here. It's what he's doing now."

Sure enough, the wind was blowing fiercely enough that both girls' hair whipped around their faces with fury. Additionally, Samantha had to hold onto the table to keep her chair still as it rocked with increasing force whereas Charlotte's barely moved and Phineas' was steady as ever.

"Okay then," Samantha said. "I guess it's safe to say that this will be a solo trip."

"It's not too late to change your mind."

Samantha shook her head and closed her eyes. "Let's do this. Help me, Charlotte."

Together, the girls combined the power of their minds to recall that day six months ago when Raven had entered Samantha's thoughts, manipulating her actions and sending her careening over a cliff. Charlotte, in turn, had been grief stricken and used her sorrow to transport herself into the Romani Realms from Samantha's gravesite, which was only a place holder as her body had also been sent into the Realms.

The sounds of the lightening overhead was replaced by the grinding of gears. As the rabbit continued to hover above the table, the sparks that erupted from its fur blew into a sudden firestorm and the creature disappeared, the dripping sound of its blood now replaced with a distinct ticking. Tick tick tick. The sound of time as it lapsed filled the air as wind moved the continuum forward and backward with Samantha's present form still seated at the table.

Instinctively, both Charlotte and Samantha retracted their hands from each other, but kept their eyes closed whereas Phineas remained all seeing and at the same time blind to the happenings before him.

As the ticking of clocks and the grinding of gears grew louder, the wind blew harder until Samantha was no longer in the present, but traveling the movement of time...back and then forward into the Romani Realms...with life and death becoming one and the same.

# # #

The massive mirror that hung over James' bar quivered and glowed with light in the darkened room revealing one black hole that threatened to swallow up the couple like a mouth seeking its last meal. With his arms around Suki's waist, James shouted over the pandemonium and tumult. "Hold on! Don't look at it," he warned, knowing that the temptation to turn toward that opening was a strong one, but it only housed soulless ones who were trapped in time.

"Why is this happening? We're together; Raven isn't here. Phineas is watching over the girls..."

"It doesn't make sense," he admitted.

However, as a Shade, James' insight was connected to Suki. Hers in turn was connected to Charlotte and Samantha. With neither detecting a problem in their wards, the situation was a bafflement.

"I think we need to get closer to them," James suggested to which Suki nodded and started immediately for the door. She didn't get far, the force field from the mirror pulling her back with rapid and dangerous speed.

"Suki!" James shouted, grabbing her just in time and pulling her once again to safety next to him. "Don't be so impetuous."

"I'm sorry. You're right. I just need a minute." Suki closed her eyes, allowing James to keep her body safe while she allowed her mind to roam and find her Releasors: Charlotte and Samantha.

"Anything?" James asked. "Concentrate, Suki. Feel them. Where are they?"

"I don't know...I can't bear to believe what I see."

"Tell me, Suki."

"I see death."

# # #

Chapter Thirty-Two

Samantha had no sooner disappeared when Phineas awoken from his trance. Charlotte threw her head against his shoulder and cried, a mournful sound that sent birds scuttling from the trees above.

"Shhhh," he soothed and ran his hand down the back of her head and through her golden hair. "Come on now. It's what she wanted and look...it worked."

"How can you be certain?" Charlotte asked, brushing her tears away with the back of her hand.

Phineas pointed to where the rabbit had rested, along with the bowl that had been under the table. Both were free of any trace of blood, as if nothing had ever happened, certainly not anything that resembled black magic.

"That's good, right?" Charlotte whispered as if not daring to jinx the situation.

"Yeah, we did it." Again, he held her close, trying to soothe her disheartened spirit for although they were successful in what they set out to do, it didn't diminish the loss they felt for their friend.

"Do you think she'll ever come back? Will she even know how?"

"Charlotte, if that was what she wanted, I don't think she would have asked for this in the first place."

Charlotte nodded, more to herself than Phineas, as if digesting the sentiment that she already knew to be true. "She wasn't herself since we had gotten back. She was distracted, almost angry in a way."

For the first time, a wiggle of doubt crept into Phineas' soul. "What do you mean? Angry? I thought it was all about missing Daniel."

"Well, yeah."

"But missing someone you love doesn't translate into anger." Phineas moved away from Charlotte, putting his hands on his hips and starting to pace the room.

"Phin, what's wrong?"

"It's just that I could understand if she seemed sad, broken-hearted, or even depressed. But anger...tell me Charlotte that she didn't just manipulate us into sending her back for some reason unknown to us."

"What in the world Phineas? You're not making sense."

"The Romani Realms can change a person, Charlotte. It breeds our worst emotions such as power, jealousy, gluttony. If you have a bit of it in you, it only manifests and grows in the Realms. I thought her only reason for going back was her love for Daniel."

Charlotte remained quiet for a moment, thinking on what Phineas had said. Finally, she asked, "Would she be able to incite the Triad with two others? I mean, it was originally meant for Samantha, Suki and myself, but then Raven thought she could use it with you and a child. What if Samantha thinks she can do the same with herself, Daniel...and Shadow?"

Phineas placed his hand under Charlotte's chin, knowing how worried she was about their unborn child, Shadow, who remained in the Realms until the time came when Charlotte became pregnant. "Shadow will be with us...when the time is right. We will have a family and she will be a part of it."

"But what if Samantha meets her again in the Realms? What if she tells Shadow that I'm not coming back? What if..."

"Shhh, Charlotte. No more 'ifs'. They're pointless."

A tear of worry dipped along Charlotte's cheek. "I just wish everything was back the way it used to be."

"Life goes forward. If wishes were horses, beggars would ride." Phineas recited an old phrase meant to ease Charlotte's fears, but it did nothing of the sort.

# # #

Chapter Thirty-Three

"There's nobody here. I'm alone," Daniel called out to the repeated pounding at his door.

The soldiers who had searched for Raven earlier had now been replaced by Buraqs. For two weeks straight they had come looking for her at the quiet cottage. But Daniel had years of experience in the Romani Realms and knew how to evade them. With a grimace he contemplated just how many years. So many, in fact, that even he had no concept of how long he had been there, but at least the time served him well. They would never find her. Not on his watch.

She had barely eluded capture. They had picked up her scent and although she managed to get back to Daniel's cottage, now his involvement with her was suspect. Tired and hungry, Raven didn't mind spending time alone in the cottage. She actually relished the moments of quiet reflection as it gave her time to consider her life, the narrow escapes, and why she had been granted the good fortune to have Daniel on her side.

She wondered if it were the master planner's way of saying he had bigger fish to fry, or if Raven was truly deserving of a second chance because of the remorse she felt for those she had harmed along the way. Either way, she was content to sit for hours if needed and ponder how to live a better life.

The freedom of flying the night skies was gladly traded in to spend time in Daniel's ingenious hiding place. She had spent so much time there recently that she finally thought to ask why it even existed. Daniel explained that many moons earlier, when food was scarce, he needed a place to hide his own supplies. He had yet to create a profitable business as a farmer. At the time, there was no bartering of services, no buying of goods, only the authorities taking what they wanted.

But times had changed when people such as Raven had come into power. She had established a more genteel Romani Realms with ballroom dances and finery, and at least the appearance of an upper class. It had served to convince those in power to start acting with some semblance of decorum if only to maintain an air of being better than others. It was ironic that now she was hiding from a siege in which she was a direct target for being overthrown.

She had said to Daniel one night over dinner, a habit they had come to enjoy together, "You can take a soul from a person, but you can't take the soulless ones from the Romani Realms." What she meant was that people...or those who were once human...will continue to pursue their desires at any cost.

As the Buraqs made their nightly rounds, Daniel decided to test the waters and speak up, after all, these same foot soldiers benefitted greatly from his most recent harvest and needed to remember that Daniel also wielded some leverage. "So, do you intend to pay me a visit every night?"

The first Buraq nodded his enormous horse head, eyeing Daniel as if noticing him for the first time in spite of being in his home repeatedly.

"In that case, do you mind coming either an hour earlier or one later? I do hate to have my dinner interrupted each evening."

The second patrolling Buraq stepped toward Daniel with a menacing gait, standing straight and trying hard to intimidate, which was typically not a difficult task given the fact that these horse-headed creatures had bodies resembling that of the strongest men. The fact that they were also extremely well hung and didn't have any modesty for their nude state also made being in their presence an uncomfortable task.

They would show off their wares as a way to tell the other males who resided in the Romani Realms that they could take their women whenever and wherever they chose. But Daniel wasn't like other men. He was equally strong, wiser than most, and had experience and patience on his side. Unlike others, he didn't mind living in the Realms for he had nothing else to live for. It placed him in a position of not desiring worldly goods and being happy and accepting of his daily existence.

When the Buraq didn't answer, Daniel gave him a swift shove behind his knees, bringing the Buraq down. Daniel placed a firm hand on the Buraq's mane and pulled backwards, forcing the creature to remain in place, staring up at Daniel in a subservient position.

"I'm not asking, actually. I'm telling you," he said, his tone quiet but firm. "For two weeks you have visited my property unannounced. You have found nothing and nobody. Your investigation is deemed over. Tell that to your council or I will cut off your produce supply. Now go!" Daniel released the Buraq, who stood up shakily, unaccustomed to having anyone treat it this way, but being a descendent of a horse, it reacted to authority and Daniel had now proven himself in this light.

The Buraq turned to leave, but in its unusually nervous condition, it tripped up on a corner of the rug. Daniel remembered back to when the foot soldier had nearly stumbled upon the hiding space in the same manner of accident. It worked once, it can work again, he promised himself.

Daniel quickly averted his eyes, not wanting to draw attention to the uneven floorboard that was now partially revealed. A moment of posturing ensued with the Buraq sizing up Daniel and deciding if it should indeed go. Daniel met its stare, placing his hands on his hips and widening his stance, but never once did he let his eyes travel to the floorboard where only inches below it, Raven waited. One sneeze. One creak of the wood chair he had placed in the crawl space and all his bravado would be for nothing.

Finally, the Buraq signaled to its counterpart and the two left the cottage and ran down the path into the woods. Daniel watched from the window to ensure they didn't turn back before going to fetch Raven.

Rolling the heavy rug away and wiggling two fingers into a groove within one of the floorboards, he pulled upwards, revealing the trap door. He heaved it upwards until the panel came loose and the small staircase leading under the house was visible. Holding up a candle, he signaled for Raven.

"That took longer than usual," she noted climbing out of the space, a tone of worry in her voice. Yet, she still smiled at Daniel as she always did when she saw his face. "Not that I'm complaining, mind you. I appreciate everything you've done for me."

"Hopefully, they won't be back."

"Daniel, don't take any stupid risks...not for me."

"What do you mean? 'Not for you' I don't offer these superior surroundings to just anybody."

"Seriously, Daniel. I heard what you did. Be careful." Raven looked him in the eye, and then, surprising both of them, tears started to slide down her cheeks. "Oh, not again. Damn, I hate how this place wreaks havoc on one's emotions. It...it doesn't mean anything."

Daniel reached a hand and ever so slowly wiped the tears off her cheek. But then, he found he didn't want to remove his hand. He couldn't bring himself to break the contact with Raven. "It's not true, you know."

"What's not true?" Raven punctuated the question with a hearty sniff and slurp of her tears.

Daniel chuckled at the display. Normally so in control of her emotions, Raven sobbed once more. "You're crying because you care for me."

"Do not!"

"Do too," he said in a child-like sing-song voice, which then turned her tears to laughter.

"You're ridiculous and full of yourself. You know that, right?"

Daniel offered her a hand and led her back to the kitchen where he had set her dinner plate in the oven to remain both out of sight of the Buraqs and maintain its warmth until she could return to it.

When she was seated and calm, tucking into his shepherd's pie with hearty spoonfuls, Daniel decided to broach the subject once more. "Raven?"

"Mmmhhm?" she mumbled, not able to tear herself away from his superior cooking.

"It's nice having someone here. It's nice having you here. And, I'll even be so bold as to say that I think you feel the same...which is why worrying about *me* brought you to tears. You can blame it on the Romani Realms, but I know better."

Raven set down her spoon. When she first turned up at Daniel's place she was severely malnourished, not having eaten more than what she could gather in the woods for the weeks that she had spent running. Needless to say, other than an intrusion by the Buraqs, it took a lot to cause her to cease eating, but Daniel had managed.

"That might have a shred of truth to it," she replied, the old Raven with her pride still strongly intact showing through.

Daniel smiled broadly and pulled her chair toward him. He gathered her up and hugged her. "I knew it!"

"What are you doing? You are crazy!" she shouted as he still held her, his arms easily wrapping around her tiny frame. "Let me go or I swear it, I'll...I'll..."

"What? Turn me into a frog? That's fairytale stuff."

Raven stomped on the ground, trying to step on Daniel's foot, although being careful to miss all the same.

"Pathetic," he said in response.

"I wasn't really trying. If I were trying, I would crush you and you'd be running straight into the swamps and to your..."

But she couldn't bring herself to utter the threat, even knowing it was an idle one. The Romani Realms were too unpredictable and she would never forgive herself if she took away someone as good as Daniel, not just from herself, but from the world.

The very thought of something happening to Daniel, either at the hands of the Buraqs or herself, nearly started her emotions bubbling to the surface again. Instead, she stopped struggling against his hold and simply placed her head on his shoulder, breathing in the woodsy scent of his neck and feeling the warmth of his body permeate her.

They had pretended to fight before, their arms holding each other down in a show to see who was stronger. With Raven's powers diminished in the Realms and Daniel's brawn, they were pretty well matched. Always, one would release the other and they would go back to the chores around the farm that kept them busy from morning to night, but this time was different.

They looked into each other's eyes at the exact same time. Any other couple would have taken this moment as that magic one, the one when a kiss occurred. But, they were both too awestruck of the situation and turned away, although Daniel didn't readily release her. When Raven awkwardly reached for her spoon, he finally set her back on her own chair.

"Sorry, I didn't realize you hadn't finished. Please do...you're still too thin."

"You know...it's kinda nice having...this."

"This?" he prompted, hoping her response would match his own thoughts.

"Having dinner with someone. Or rather, having someone to have dinner with. Won't you eat with me? You couldn't have had much yourself before we were so rudely interrupted."

"When you put it that way, how can I refuse? I'll just grab my bowl." Daniel left the table to retrieve his bowl from the kitchen. He looked over his shoulder at Raven and smiled to himself.

# # #

Daniel ladled another helping of stew into Raven's bowl. The bread that had been baking in the oven had just come out, its aroma filling the cottage. Neither wasted a moment or needed an excuse for second helpings. Raven broke off a chunk, blowing on her fingertips as the steam vapored into the air and then promptly dunked the slice into her bowl, absorbing the rich, dark gravy.

"This is delicious. It reminds me of a dish my mother used to make."

"You had a mother?"

Raven elbowed him in the ribs playfully. "Of course I had a mother."

Daniel blushed with his faux pas. "That's not what I meant. I just...I don't know."

"Didn't think I was capable of giving or receiving love?"

"Something like that." He smiled widely, his irresistible dimples prominent. The facial feature gave him a look of innocence and Raven couldn't fault him for the jibe. Still, she wasn't going to let the comment be swept under the rug.

"I actually had a pretty good childhood. Things got screwed up as I got older..." she explained, and then elaborated, "men."

"Don't go blaming the entire species. I'm the good guy in the story."

Raven put down her spoon, now completely satiated by the meal. Looking at Daniel, she nodded. "Yeah...you are."

In that moment Raven wondered if the tricks that played upon one's mind in the Romani Realms were haunting her at this very moment for she felt something pass between herself and Daniel that she had never felt before – hope. He honestly seemed to be falling for her. This couldn't be described as ego for she had centuries of success in being able to seduce any man she fancied. This was different because she felt the same. It had nothing to do with her mind and everything to do with her heart. She happily finished off her stew sending off a silent prayer that love could actually bloom in the Romani Realms.

# # #

Chapter Thirty-Four

Suki placed two fingers on her temple, trying to ward off the headache that was accosting her. Uneasy thoughts of her Releasors wreaked havoc with her psyche. She had been attuned to them since they released her from her bottle, but in the subsequent months migraines only struck when danger did.

"Just breathe," James instructed. He had watched over Suki for centuries and always knew what she was feeling, but this was worse than usual. "You need to focus and determine who is at risk."

"I know. We're not going to have a repeat of my gravest error." Suki spoke of the time when Raven had manipulated her thoughts into believing that Charlotte was in great danger when in reality it was Samantha who was nearing a cliff's edge and ultimately, plummeted.

James took Suki's hands in his own, gently running his thumbs over them in a rhythmic motion. "That's better," he said softly as her breathing began to settle.

"Let's do this," she said, her voice anxious, her tone still pitched with pain.

"It's important that you get control of the pain first. Here, let me help." Concentrating on her, James forced his own positive thoughts into her, letting the energy wash from himself and into her. Their hands warmed, their inhalations matched each other, and soon he heard Suki sigh audibly.

"Better?" he asked.

She nodded.

"Okay then. This death that you speak of, has it occurred? Can you see Charlotte or Samantha?"

"They're alive," she confirmed. "But I see the bleakness of lost hope and souls who have passed on, but are..." Suki shook her head, struggling for the right word, before finally completing her thought. "Stuck. They're just in limbo."

"You know that sounds like the Romani Realms," James said evenly, trying hard not to make himself or Suki jump to conclusions. "Let's just stay calm. Do you see anything else that might lead us to them?"

"Only throngs of soulless ones, walking through dark forests. The hands reaching out of the murky mud, struggling to pull themselves out...or someone else down. But then the vision fades."

Suki's trauma was starting to affect James as well. He closed his eyes for a moment before opening them again, trying to stave off the effects of how Suki's Releasors were bringing her discomfort and in turn, him as well while he held her hands. "Suki, it just doesn't make sense. You can only see visions pertaining to your Releasors."

Suki's eyes opened widely with recognition. "Not just visions of them, but also surrounding them. I see what they see. Oh my god, James. We have to go to the place where Samantha was last seen."

James looked at her with bewilderment. "The very last place?" he questioned.

Suki nodded. "The site of her funeral. Now!"

# # #

Chapter Thirty-Five

T he following morning Daniel awoke early to go
into the town center for more supplies. As a
farmer, he was used to waking early to tend his crops
in order to put in a number of hours before the
midday sun's heat forced him to take refuge inside for
an extended lunch. But lately he had spent at least
one morning a week to venture away from his farm,
not only to make purchases, but also to hear any
gossip that might relate to Raven's disappearance.

They still hoped that she would be able to gain
favor among the people of the Romani Realms, but
for the moment the insurgents who had overthrown
those in power were still wielding too much influence
on the weak. Fortunately, both Raven and Daniel had
come to create a positive out of a bad situation. He
felt whole having someone share his life and found
himself wanting to hurry back to her the moment he
left. On days like today when the talk in the town
wasn't good, he felt especially anxious about leaving
her alone.

He returned to find her enjoying the morning
sunshine, sipping her coffee on one of the Adirondack
chairs behind his house. Although the seating area

she enjoyed was down a winding path that meandered from the house and deep into the field that he tended, if someone were nosy enough they could certainly venture out far enough to discover her.

"Raven, it's not safe for you to be out in the open."

"I'm not in the open. I'm back here."

"Never mind. We don't have time to argue. Come back inside," he said extending his hand to her and helping her up from the low chair.

When they got back inside, Daniel's quiet mood made Raven nervous and she started to move about the cottage busying herself with mundane tasks. She fluffed the pillows on the couch, straightened the cushions, then started to refresh a vase of flowers by pulling off the dead leaves and petals.

"Stop. Just come and sit with me," Daniel called from the couch that was covered in a sunny pattern of yellow and blue plaid that was considerably happier than his mood. "Why are you in perpetual motion?"

"Because you're not saying anything and it's making me nervous. What's wrong?"

"I think either Charlotte or Samantha is coming back. Maybe both. Could be they're already here." Daniel just blurted it out.

"Wow, you don't hold back." Raven sank down onto the couch and just stared at the wall in front of her. It was quite possibly the worst news she had ever heard, more upsetting even than learning about the uprising because if it were true, she had much more to lose. Daniel.

"What did you hear?" she finally asked in a small voice.

"The soulless ones have been talking about what they plan to do when Charlotte and Samantha return. They didn't actually say they were here. Maybe it's just wishful thinking."

Raven turned to him with an expression that indicated he must be crazy.

"That's not what I meant," Daniel backpedaled. "*I'm* not wishing for it."

In Raven's mind, the timing of this news couldn't be worse. She felt an intimacy with Daniel that she had never experienced with another man. But now, fears of losing him surfaced.

"Raven, I'm not going to leave you."

"How do you do that? You don't have special powers."

He pulled her in close and nuzzled her neck while tickling her mercilessly. "Because I've come to know you. For the last few weeks, we've spent every day and every night together. And let me tell you...you're pretty amazing."

She pursed her lips together as if trying hard not to say the words that were desperate to come out. Daniel saw her internal struggle and did his best to put her mind at ease.

"Raven, you won't lose me...if that's what concerns you."

The old Raven would protest and insist that the thought never entered her mind. Too proud to admit to needing someone, she would normally never show her vulnerabilities. But her time with Daniel had changed her. "You sure?"

He nodded. "Besides, this is all just talk."

"But what if it isn't just talk? What if she were here right now?"

"She?"

"Daniel, you know what I'm getting at."

"They spoke of Charlotte too."

Raven crossed her arms. "Charlotte isn't a threat to me."

"And an ordinary girl like Samantha is?"

"Would you still feel the same about her? The way you used to?" she asked, ignoring the rhetorical question he had posed.

"She has no way of getting back. She's mortal, and alive again."

"You didn't answer me. Would you love her again?"

Daniel noticed that Raven had placed a distance between the two of them. He patted the cushion beside him, indicating he wanted her near. When she complied, he answered with seriousness. "That's a hard question."

"I guess that's your answer." Raven stood and stormed around the cottage locating some of her clothes and throwing them into a bag.

"Raven, I want you to stay. If Samantha were here...well, let's just say that you probably wouldn't care for me if I were the type of guy to not care about what happens to her. Think about that."

Raven stopped the small tantrum she had allowed herself and came back to join Daniel once again. He was right, of course. She knew she could trust him and that loyalty was a part of him. He wasn't the type of man to turn it on and off when it pleased him.

"You're right. It's your goodness that is so attractive. But that doesn't mean I'm not...oh my God I can't believe I'm even thinking this...the only word to describe how I feel is insecure. This place sucks."

She fiddled with the bag of clothes that were at her feet as if still trying to decide whether or not to make a run for it and save her heart.

He laughed in spite of her seriousness and pulled her close to him. "Raven? I can tell you this. Right now, I'm with you. So stay with me. It's not safe for you out there."

"But if she came back, you'd rush to help her."

"Maybe, but only to keep her from being attacked," he admitted. "I'll always be honest with you. She was the first bright spot in this place, but that doesn't diminish what I feel for you. I love that you've opened yourself up to me. You have goodness in you and for me to be able to release that...it's quite an ego boost."

He reached his arms around her back and pulled her against his chest. When he finally heard her sigh, releasing the stress that had built up within her, he placed a hand under her chin and forced her to look deep into his eyes. There was nothing else to say, no words were necessary, but he decided that actions were important and so, he kissed her.

With a sideways smile, she seductively said, "Well, here's to stroking your...ego."

Daniel didn't say a word. He merely led her to his bedroom.

# # #

Chapter Thirty-Six

Suki swiped at the tears trailing her cheeks, her long, dark lashes still wet from the worry that plagued her. She whispered a quiet prayer. "Please don't let us be too late."

"We're going to take the fast train for this trip. Hold onto me," James stated and took Suki by the wrist.

"No, not that. I need to be strong when we arrive. It's like I get the bends and feel nauseous every time we go..."

But Suki never got her final words out. The air in the bar stirred slowly at first and then grew more powerful. Gale force gusts blew at her hair and lifted her skirt. Chairs tipped over and napkins scattered. And then, the familiar creaking of the clocks of time could be heard along with bells sounding their departure from one time dimension into another.

One of the smaller, wooden chairs was pulled into the twirling funnel of wind. Its leg whacked Suki against the back of her head and she would have slumped to the ground had James not been by her side still holding her hand. He pulled her up and shouted above the melee. "Close your eyes. Just concentrate on the destination. You're fighting it and the winds of time are moving against us."

More furniture flew into the air, floorboards started to buckle and Suki cried out when it seemed the wind would tear the place to the ground. "James!"

"We'll be okay."

He held her tightly against his strong chest seemingly not affected by what felt like a mini hurricane. With one hand placed on the small of her back and the other against the back of her head, James embraced Suki and protected her small frame.

"That's it," he said in her ear. "We'll be on our way."

The mirror opened up and turned to black as James and Suki were sucked into a portal that transported them to where Phineas still stood holding Charlotte as if no time had passed for them whatsoever.

# # #

"You okay? I'm sorry it was such a fast ride. There was no time to waste," James said to her.

"I'm just peachy keen." Suki was seated on the ground holding her head, obviously struggling to get her bearings in spite of her words to the contrary. She gazed up at James who looked absolutely majestic as he stood tall, his frame blocking the midday sun making him seem almost angelic as the rays glowed behind him. "How is it that you look like you just stepped off of a modeling shoot?"

"Must be the windswept hair look." Phineas' voiced sounded and they turned to see him and Charlotte approach.

But this wasn't a happy homecoming. Suki fought the affects of the time travel and stood up to address them. Her Southern mannerisms were forgotten, replaced by a fear that took away her gentility. "This is a disgusting place to be hanging out," she motioned to the head stones of the old cemetery where they had landed. "What are you doing here?" Suki demanded.

They looked at James and Suki a bit guiltily. "Answer her!" James shouted. "We can't waste any time. Not if her visions are correct."

Phineas placed his arm around James' shoulders and tried to lead him away. "Let's allow Charlotte to speak to Suki alone," he said.

"No! I don't want him to leave," Suki shouted. "Just tell me what you have to say."

"Samantha is gone," Charlotte said quietly. "We did as she wanted," she added quickly.

Her explanation of the recent events were no sooner out of her mouth when Suki broke down and cried.

James' reaction was just as fast and with a swift punch, he decked Phineas in the jaw.

"What the fuck, man?" Phineas rubbed his jaw, the redness forming fast. "It's like Charlotte said. We only did what Samantha asked," Phineas shouted. "It's not like we wanted to say goodbye, but she was insistent. She hated being without him."

"You'll get her killed. Maybe Charlotte too," James shouted back with equal force.

Phineas quieted. "What are you talking about?"

James paced in a circle, then hit his forehead with his palms in frustration. "You have no idea what you've done."

Suki approached, her tears stopped flowing with the testosterone surged scene that had unfolded before them. "The Realms will pull us all to her. We are all bonded to each other and you know that I am connected to both of you. If she is there, I'll certainly follow and I'll end up pulling Charlotte there too."

James spoke up, "And you, lover boy, will end up there if Charlotte's there."

"And you'll be there if Suki is there..." Phineas said quietly. The anger among the crowd had dissipated, now replaced by a deep dread.

"What now?" Charlotte asked.

"We wait. Wait and try to fight the temptation to be returned." James' look was grave. "Because when it strikes you, and it will, I don't know what will save you."

# # #

Chapter Thirty-Seven

Daniel and Raven slept with arms and legs entangled around each other, and when they awoke in the morning Daniel layered kisses over Raven's lips once more. Speaking against her mouth, he murmured, "We should just stay in this room for the rest of the day."

"Mmm, I'd like that," came her muffled reply.

"Sadly, there are crops calling to me." Daniel disentangled himself from Raven's loving embrace. Planting one last kiss on her forehead, he got up from the bed and grabbed a pair of jeans that was left hanging over a chair.

Raven smiled and signed a deep, happy breath and rolled onto her back in what she thought would be a few minutes more of sleep. Contentedness fast turned to discomfort and she gasped in shock while moving her fingers to her temples.

The pain gave way to a vision, one that she may have welcomed months earlier but now only served to fill her with apprehension. Phineas. She saw her former lover and protege, no doubt because she had given him lasting life and was therefore bonded to him for the duration of that life.

He was still handsome. Perhaps even more so than he had been while they were together as he had matured a bit around the eyes, his shoulders were a bit broader than she remembered, and his hair had a just woken quality that was sexier than sin.

Still, she didn't want him. She didn't want that life back. The manipulation that came with controlling Phineas and her quest for power was exhausting, although at the time she didn't recognize it as anything other than duty to herself and the price that must be paid for injustices she faced.

So why was she seeing images of Phineas as Daniel still stood before her? She turned her attention to her new love, happy to appraise his physique, which was just as appealing as Phineas'. Her eyes fluttered to Daniel's chest and moved down the defined muscle tone of his stomach. She couldn't help that her eyes didn't stop there. It was impossible to not notice the indentation of his muscles that formed a V and insisted that her attention be directed to the region which was now being zipped up within Daniel's jeans.

"You okay? You've got a funny look on your face."

Raven blushed, caught in her own perverted thoughts. "Fine. I'm good. Really good."

He looked at her with amusement. "I'll see you later."

Daniel was just turning to go when again Raven gasped, this time the headache strong enough to make her fall back against the pillows.

"Raven? What's wrong?"

"I don't know...the pain...it's so intense," she wailed, bringing her hands to cover her eyes. "And the room...it's so bright."

Daniel lay down beside her and shielded her eyes with his hand as he gently petted her hair, pushing it back from her forehead in what he hoped was a soothing gesture. When he stopped, Raven grabbed his hand back. "Don't stop. It's helping."

"Better?" His voice was tender and filled with concern.

"Yeah," she said opening her eyes and pulling herself up to a seated position.

"You sure?"

Raven looked around the room as if she half expected the walls to come crumbling down on her. When nothing happened and still her head remained free of pain, she answered. "I saw something I wasn't expecting. A vision of the past. Or maybe...the future?"

"I take it this vision involved someone you know?" Daniel narrowed his eyes.

"Phineas," she admitted.

Daniel paused and Raven watched his expression. Both waited before speaking, each trying their best not to overreact as their relationship was still young.

Raven couldn't remain silent any longer. "Say something. You're mad."

But Daniel merely shook his head. "Nah, I couldn't get mad at you. Especially since the very idea of Phineas gives you a headache."

Relieved, she reached her arms around his neck and kissed him on the cheek.

"He's probably a pain in the ass too." Daniel kissed her back, letting his mouth find hers.

"Didn't you say something about crops not being able to harvest themselves?"

"Shh..." he nuzzled her neck. "It can wait." He pulled back the covers and pushed Raven onto them. The two met in a heap as the sound of a rooster crowing beckoned, but was ignored.

# # #

Chapter Thirty-Eight

"I'm sorry, Suki." Charlotte pleaded for forgiveness. "You must know that we were only trying to ease her pain."

"By sending her back there? There of all places? How can that ease anyone's pain? That place is full of misery."

Phineas and Charlotte didn't answer. They couldn't. There was no denying the truth behind Suki's words. They had all experienced the desolate bleakness of the Romani Realms, filled with its desperate souls and vile creatures.

It seemed asinine that Suki had to verbalize it. "I know you can only see the craziness of us wanting to send her back," Charlotte agreed, "but...when someone is so miserable here, well...she wasn't herself here."

"We honestly felt that we were helping," Phineas added, placing a protective arm around Charlotte. "Please don't take it out on Charlotte."

"Why?" Suki snapped in an uncharacteristically harsh voice. "Was this your idea?"

"No! Suki, he had nothing to do with it. Phineas tried to talk us out of it."

Suki paced back and forth, running her hands through her hair. "I have to go and get her."

"You can't do that, Suki," James spoke for the first time since the argument began. "It's starting. You have to fight it."

"I'm not leaving her," Suki responded. "This is my decision! It's not the pull of the Realms."

"You say that, but...I'm just asking, please think this through..." James replied carefully as if not wanting to state what was obvious to him.

"I'm not following you," Suki said.

James took her hands in his, cradling them...wanting to take away the pain that he would no doubt cause with his words. "Samantha is your Releasor and no doubt, she will need you..."

"Which is why I need to go, right away!"

"Suki..." Charlotte spoke softly, the realization hitting her first. "It's very easy to make wishes in the Romani Realms...reality is distorted, and Samantha may not realize the impact."

"Oh Charlotte," Suki left James' side to go to Charlotte, "that won't happen." The realization of what harm Samantha could inflict now registering in Suki's mind. Still, she didn't want to believe it. Like a mother protecting her young, Suki could not fathom that Samantha might wish for harm to come to any of them simply because she wanted to stay in the Romani Realms. "You have to trust her."

Charlotte looked down and Suki realized how impossible the situation had grown. Of course they trusted Samantha; they just couldn't fault her for what she might do. Too many people before them had wished for death rather than be haunted by the atrocities of the Realms.

Suki knew it as well, and whispered in James' ear. "I won't see you again."

He grabbed her shoulders with force and shook his head, too moved to even speak.

"Yes, James." Her voice was calm as if a million scenarios had run through her mind already and she had chosen. She knew the answer, even if he refused to acknowledge it.

"Suki..." James' voice was a low warning. "Don't be stubborn. It's not the time."

"This isn't about getting my own way. It's about commitment and responsibility. And trust."

Charlotte and Phineas watched their argument unfold. "What are you talking about?" Charlotte spoke up.

"She's being ridiculous," James answered. "She thinks that her responsibility to Samantha trumps everything. Even you, Charlotte!"

"That's a low blow, James. I'm not choosing Samantha over Charlotte. Honestly, darlin', I'm not." Suki took Charlotte's hands in her own. "It's just that she has Phineas here to protect her and frankly, there really isn't any threat to her. Raven isn't here. The Romani Realms aren't here. But Samantha..." her voice trailed off. "Samantha is entering dangerous territory and you all have to trust that I can fend for myself."

She paused while nobody answered and then, in an attempt to persuade them, she did the opposite. "Besides, if Samantha uses her last wish, then it was meant to be, and you'll all go on and be fine without me."

James formed a fist with one hand and pounded it into his palm, frustration showing on his face. "That's not going to happen."

"Frankly darlin' you don't have a say in the matter." Suki raised her eyebrows and stood proud, daring him to argue. She may have been born and raised with Southern gentility, but that didn't exclude her from being a feminist. When she made up her mind, neither high water nor a man could convince her otherwise.

James knew when he was beat. "You know what I have to say to that? I'm coming with you."

"But James, maybe you're coming for the wrong reasons."

He wrinkled his brow and gave Suki a look as if she were crazy. "Suki, I'm your Shade. How can protecting you be the wrong reason?"

"It's like you said, maybe it's the pull getting to us. First me, then you...just let me go. It's for the best."

"No you don't. You're forgetting that I love you," he placed a finger over her lips, silencing the argument right out of her.

Charlotte and Phineas joined them, forming a circle. "We're in." Charlotte placed her arm around Suki's waist.

"What? No!" Suki started to protest. "No way. Not again."

"Sorry, kid," Phineas smiled, his boyish charm oozing through his dimples. "You're stuck with us. And this isn't the pull of the Realms talking."

James held out his hand to Phineas, who gripped it tightly and then pulled James in for a no holds barred hug. When the two men separated, the foursome stared at each other and then Phineas held his fist into the circle. The four bumped their knuckles against each other and then no sooner pulled their hands away with fingers spread, like birds in flight.

Suki was the first to speak. "I don't condone any of you going back to that forsaken place, but I can't deny that having you by my side..." she paused, tears coming to her eyes. "Are you sure about this?" She looked from one to the other.

"You're not going alone, Suki," James spoke first, taking her in his arms. It took less than a second for Phineas and Charlotte to jump on that hug, wrapping their arms around Suki and James' back, holding on and squeezing like best friends do.

Suki turned to give each one their own hug. "You guys are insane. But, I think that's what I love about you most."

# # #

Chapter Thirty-Nine

R aven tilted her head upwards and Daniel didn't miss the opportunity to meet her lips with his own. The kiss was soft and tender as had been all of their interactions. Raven sensed Daniel holding back. It was amusing to her that a man should behave so cautiously, almost carefully with her. She was, after all, quite capable of taking care of herself. Yet, having someone worry about her was perhaps more appealing than any seduction. She felt her need grow and wanted to scream against his mouth that she desired him.

Wanting to show him that she was worthy of his affections, that she was a lady, Raven attempted to focus her mind elsewhere. Teen boys often spoke of mentally running through the multiplication tables in order to stave off their reaction. She now realized the usefulness of that advice.

Try as she might to maintain her cool while making out with Daniel, his hand resting at her lower back created not only a stirring, but a struggle. How she wanted him. Last night was like an appetizer and she was hungry for the main course. She arched her back, trying to encourage his hand to move lower without, of course, seeming as if that were her intention.

Her head was dizzy from the intensity of her feelings and she pulled her mouth away, lifted her chin and drew Daniel's attention to her graceful neck. When his mouth traced kisses from below her ear to the hollow of her throat, she couldn't remain silent.

"Oh god," her fingers dug into his back as thoughts of what else he could do with that mouth swam in her head.

"I could kiss you forever."

"No..."

"No?" His tone was playful and suddenly Raven knew that she was being teased...mercilessly so.

"I need more...Daniel, please."

His loving attention stopped only long enough to allow him to caress the side of her face and whisper in her ear. "Why didn't you say so sooner? Your wish...my command."

Daniel pulled his shirt over his head and stared down at Raven as he prepared to take their loving farther. She had never felt more desire toward anyone, but there was a time when she would have chosen power over love. His words, although meant to be a cute declaration, brought with them a reminder of Raven's past.

As she stared into Daniel's eyes, his image morphed into that of Phineas and her ears rang with a grinding, industrial noise. On the wind, the sound of gears moving could be heard along with something else...Suki's voice. It was soft and lyrical as it spoke to her Releasors. "Your wish...my command."

Raven gasped, which Daniel believed indicated her rising passion. His leg nudged hers apart and she complied seeing his face once more. She inhaled deeply, trying to steady her faltering emotions. Running her hand over Daniel's chiseled abs, she relaxed into the moment. But when her hands continued to explore his body, moving up his arms, she saw Phineas once more, his biceps, not Daniel's. Phineas' chest, abdomen, and more.

As Daniel's hand traveled down her thigh, she was transported back to her bedroom in Malibu and the last time she and Phineas were intimate. She tried to be present, knowing it was a trick of the Romani Realms. It was certainly possible to still be connected to Phineas, but never did she expect it to surface at such an inconvenient time. With every touch from Daniel, she remembered Phineas as if he were there with her. Sight and sounds, even smells were of Phineas and try as she might to get back to the present, she couldn't.

It was neither tender nor beautiful. Her relationship with Phineas wasn't built on such sentiments. It was physical and full of need. Sex had been demanding and unforgiving. Hard and sometimes angry. It took them to heights beyond what mortals experienced only to leave them breathless and unable to offer any more.

Although Daniel was merely kissing the back of her neck, his hand moving tantalizingly over her lower back, an orgasm built within her. Burying her head in the pillow, the force rocked her but she remained stoic, never letting Daniel know what had occurred. The moment it was over she felt empty.

Extreme sorrow filled her soul as Raven somehow felt she had cheated on Daniel. In that moment, she knew how much she had come to love him. So much so that the idea of doing anything to hurt him was unforgivable. They were ready to make love, yet Raven felt as if casual sex with another man had occurred. A single tear slowly rolled down her cheek.

"What is it?" Daniel rolled to the side of Raven, but didn't break contact. Cupping her chin in his hand, he kissed the tip of her nose. "We don't have to do this."

"It's not you. It's me. I want you, Daniel. And, I do love you."

A look of relief washed over his face. "Then what's wrong?"

"I'm scared."

To hear a woman with Raven's strength, her power, and the supernatural elements she controls admit to such a human foible was not what he expected. He remained silent, but cradled Raven against his chest.

Closing her eyes, she inhaled his scent, clean and woodsy like a forest of prominent pines. "You smell so good," she snuggled her cheek next to him and inadvertently ran her hand across his chest.

Her touch moved him and he closed his eyes, sighing deeply. "Raven?"

"Yes?" She propped herself up on her elbow, worried of what she might see in his expression. It felt like her relationship with Daniel was always one step forward and two steps back.

"We can go back to the way we were." He tilted his head toward the bed they now shared, although until recently, time spent there had been platonic. Their close proximity was so he could care for her to ensure that the Buraqs didn't arrive unexpectedly one night. It seemed as if the role had cemented their relationship and only recently had their sleeping arrangement led to romance.

"This is ironic. I can't believe myself." Raven shook her head and then brought a hand up to her forehead to make a show of smacking herself across it.

He laughed. "How so?"

"Because I worried that I would be the one to corrupt you. You're so good." Her sentiment was more a complaint than a compliment and the irony wasn't lost on Daniel.

"Thank you. I think," he joked, noting her tone.

"I don't want to ruin this. I messed up everything with Phineas. I hurt him and in the end...well, I think he hates me."

"I'm sure he doesn't hate you. You can't hate someone that you have so much history with."

Raven took a moment to study Daniel's expression, an understanding of the deeper meaning behind his words hitting her. History. There's no escaping the past. Neither hers nor his could be denied.

She didn't want to mention Samantha, nor ask if he still had feelings for her, but the thought was inescapable. "I want to move forward. I don't want this to end."

Again, her hand moved in small circles over his chest. He closed his eyes, relishing the feel of her hand, and then when he could resist her no longer, he pressed his own hand over hers, and guided it lower down his stomach, and then lower still.

Feeling his hardness within his trousers, Raven sighed. "Oh god. I want you." She looked at Daniel and nodded slightly, putting more power behind her words.

He didn't want to rush her. Something was pulling her in two directions, but he saw the desire in her eyes. He rolled over so that he hovered above her and bent his head so that his lips brushed her cheeks, moving along her jawline and scattering feather light caresses across her neck. If she wanted to stop, she would tell him. But Raven remained silent.

His mouth drifted down to her shoulder and as he lowered the spaghetti strap of her nightie, his hand cupped her breast, again with more tenderness than she had ever known.

Raven was well aware that reality could shift and change at any moment. She opened her eyes and saw that Daniel's remained closed. A small crease crossed his brow showing how deep into the moment he was. She inhaled deeply, relishing the feel of him as well as the knowledge that he brought her such pleasure, both mentally and physically. She wanted him with all her heart and so she opened her legs and wrapped one around his lower back, pulling at him and telling him in her way that everything was alright.

Tenderly he entered her and she gasped with the instant pleasure that filled her. Their movements remained slow and controlled as if they were savoring every moment together. There was no need to rush.

I love being with you," he pressed gently against her. His hand found hers, their fingers wove together.

For the first time in Raven's long existence she understood the real meaning of the phrase making love.

As they climaxed, the entire house shook. Windows rattled; dishes fell.

Daniel was the first to speak. "Wow, now I can sincerely say that you have rocked my world."

But Raven looked worried. "I didn't do that."

Daniel grew serious. "Then what was it?"

"I think the Romani Realms has a new arrival."

"That doesn't happen every time."

Raven shook her head, although agreeing with his observation. Instinctively, she knew the situation wasn't one that was preferable. "No, it only happens when it's someone of importance...someone they've been waiting for."

Perhaps it was sheer surprise mixed with his sudden understanding, but Daniel suddenly spoke without the ability to filter his thoughts. And the one word he uttered made Raven's heart break.

"Samantha."

# # #

Chapter Forty

Samantha's arrival was similar to the last time. She woke in the meadow, just a small walk beyond the theater in the round – the same one where she had met Daniel six months earlier. Windows surrounded the amphitheater type structure and she knew to avoid being seen as the building was home to special events for the Romani Realms' high council and its more powerful residents. As beautiful and tempting as it appeared with the smell of food calling to her, she knew to avoid it.

"I don't need to alert the officials that I'm here just yet," she mused to herself. The last time Samantha was in the Realms, Raven and the other officials on the council met within this same theater. Samantha had a plan and getting caught before she could execute it was not in the cards.

She looked across the meadow in the opposite direction, spying the swamplands in the distance where the soulless ones lied in wait. Buried in the muddy grounds, they preyed on anyone who passed.

"They can't hurt me if I don't let my mind go to them," she said to herself and with determination, turned in the direction of the swamps.

# # #

From her previous time in the Romani Realms, Samantha knew that Daniel's cottage sat at the edge of the fields that he tended. Those fields were on the outskirts of the swampland and the trek to get to them was perilous. It kept him safe and made his property a haven in the midst of this forbidden land.

Samantha crossed the meadows toward the forest that led to the swamps. She had come prepared, planning this journey for months prior with a simple plan to keep her mind occupied as she walked. For months before leaving Los Angeles, Charlotte asked her to accompany her on shopping trips and girls' luncheons, but Samantha denied every request preferring to spend her time learning the chants that she would speak to the soulless ones to keep them quiet or reading books in which the plot could be recalled at the right moments – times when her mind needed to be occupied.

Charlotte worried that her insistence on being alone was a sign of Samantha's depression. In reality, it was a concerted effort on Samantha's part to fill her mind with information that she could recall and lose herself in, rather than become prone and vulnerable to the tricks that the Romani Realms could play on one's mind.

As she walked, she thought about the plot of a Nicholas Sparks novel she had read and then seen the movie adaptation. It was typical of his work in that a woman was running from something in her past toward a man who would provide a more promising future. Yet, it was a satisfying read that filled weeks of Samantha's days and nights, carrying her thoughts to Daniel and their inevitable reunion.

A twinge of nerves struck her as she recalled the moments of the book that weren't smooth sailing for the couple in love, but she brushed the negativity aside knowing that her thoughts needed to be strong. Although her mind wandered for only a minute, it was enough of a gap to cause doubt to creep in.

She passed children playing on a swing set, an eerie tune that sounded akin to an old-fashioned merry-go-round sounded from above even though there was no sign of speakers anywhere. Children's laughter, although typically a happy sound, filled her with fear. She stopped and turned in a circle, trying to find her bearings as she expected to already have reached the forest and swamps, but found herself once again facing the amphitheater.

Each time she turned away from the building to walk in the other direction, it would appear in front of her again. Like the merry-go-round that remained invisible, she was on a virtual circular course, never-ending regardless of how far she walked. In defeat, with the memories of more pleasant books and movies long forgotten, her practiced chants escaping her mind, she sat down with head in hands accepting that she would be forced to wait for what the officials of the Romani Realms had in store for her.

When nobody approached, she decided to walk toward the group of children at play. They swung higher and higher on the swings, ignoring her questions of whether any of the officials were near. One child dressed in old-fashioned garb called out to her, "Maybe you should go inside."

"Yes, go inside," another shouted.

Samantha looked toward the theater ruefully. She didn't want the memories to flood back too soon. Daniel holding her. The two of them dancing. And Raven. Always Raven putting an end to everything. Even her friendship with Charlotte had become strained because of Raven. It was actually due to her hooking up with Phineas, but Charlotte would never have met him had Raven not tasked him with trying to get close to Charlotte.

Samantha shook her head, still not understanding how her friend could trust him. She never let on how she really felt once they got home. Sure, Charlotte acted the same way toward her, but all along, Samantha couldn't fully forgive her for being with Phineas. After all, he was one side of the coin that sent her to the Romani Realms in the first place. Samantha swiped at tears as the memory of what it was like when she first died and was resurrected here.

"Maybe I should thank Raven when I see her," she said aloud, and just as quickly as the tears emerged, her own laughter ensued as she realized that she actually owed her relationship with Daniel to Raven.

"Might as well face the music." Samantha called to anyone willing to listen, knowing that the officials heard and saw everything. With no answer and no indication of anyone coming for her, she turned once more to the children. But upon seeing them, Samantha screamed in terror at the sight that greeted her eyes.

The children, who moments earlier had flown on swings, now hung by their necks from gallows. The horrific sight made her retch. She started running, but heard noises coming for her. Looking over her shoulder, she ran and stumbled, heading toward the theater that she had desperately wanted to avoid. She moved as fast as she could, picking herself up when she stumbled and fell. The first door was ajar and she bolted through it thinking nothing of the fact that moments earlier it was closed.

# # #

Chapter Forty-One

The empty theater echoed with the sound of Samantha's footsteps as she ran without any idea of what she sought. The main room remained as she had remembered it, and when her accelerated heart rate finally got the best of her, she stopped to catch her breath and tentatively looked around. Unlike the images of the children that still soiled her mind, the round forum was beautiful with ornate gold and mahogany wood. Floor to ceiling murals of women taking tea or men riding horses during a fox hunt were reminiscent of civilized times.

But her quiet frame of mind was only momentary. The feeling of relaxation lapsed making Samantha once again uneasy. She moved through the darkened theater, feeling her way around the room by staying close to the perimeter walls. The sound of laughter propelled her toward one side of the room, although she found nobody there. A song began to play, its music soft and rhythmic, reminding her once again of dancing with Daniel in this very room. She wondered if the thought was deliberately placed in her mind. It was worrisome that even beautiful music could be used to manipulate her. The very idea was infuriating since she was the one who held a plan to control her current circumstance.

She focused her thoughts on the beauty of the music and as she relaxed, she stopped to take in the pieces of art on display. Other than the art, which were subtly illuminated, the room remained in darkness until a strobe was directed overhead at Samantha. Like the art pieces, she was on full display.

A mirror on the far side of the room caught her attention, but the reflection was dishonest. Looking down at herself, she confirmed that she was wearing the same outfit as she had upon leaving the present – a simple pair of jeans, low boots and a t-shirt. The mirrored image of herself, however, displayed a completely different girl – this one beautiful and sophisticated dressed in a gold gown that complimented her fiery mane of hair that flowed past her shoulders as opposed to the pony tail that she wore for the journey.

Samantha squinted to get a better look, but the laughter grew louder and strobe lights became more frequent, causing her to lose her perception. A stilted, mechanical voice broke the silence as it boomed from hidden speakers.

"For your viewing pleasure we present our rendition of The Four Seasons. Here in the Romani Realms better known as the pendulum of our emotions: Confusion, Anger, Lust, and Resolve. This showing will be broadcast on closed circuit television throughout the Romani Realms. There is no need to leave your homes. Consider this our holiday gift to you."

The speaker buzzed as the voice signed off and all was quiet. Samantha, still cloaked in darkness, felt her way along the walls once more. "There are doors at the end of the ballroom," she whispered to herself. "Just find the doors."

Her quest was derailed as a strong vibration hit the floor boards forcing her off balance as the floor seemed to rise and fall. Theater spotlights shone harshly on her as she tripped and applause rang out.

"Confusion!" the voice announced...and surely enough, Samantha's uneasy expression matched the declaration.

# # #

Chapter Forty-Two

In spite of their all for one attitude, once Charlotte returned to the home she now shared with Phineas, the pending reality of their upcoming trip filled her with dread. Normally, she would prepare dinner while listening to one of her favorite food television shows. Invariably, Phineas would come into the kitchen to help or as she teased, to hinder her efforts by snacking on anything she was in the midst of preparing.

Sometimes they would imitate the chefs who were becoming rising celebrities due to their television appearances. Other times, Charlotte and Phineas preferred to do the opposite, pretending to be the world's worst chefs by launching into a food fight that always ended up in the shower followed by their love making.

Tonight they were silent.

"Will you please say something?" Phineas implored.

"What is there to say? It's...well...it just is what it is." Charlotte slammed the refrigerator shut and threw a zucchini onto the counter, her displeasure growing as it broke apart with the thud she had forced on it.

"Damn it, Charlotte! Get mad at me. Yell. Scream. Just get it off your chest."

She turned to face him, hands on hips. "I should be saying the same to you. You warned me not to do as Samantha wanted. Look where we are now."

Phineas ran his hand through his hair. "I gave you the tools to send her back. I wasn't strong. I caved the moment you asked me too...just as I used to do for Raven."

Charlotte swung around, her golden hair flying behind her. "Did you just compare me to her? The women who took Samantha's life and sent her to the Romani Realms in the first place? The same person who orchestrated your death just so she could have a playmate throughout time? Don't you even go there. You'll always be half demon and it's rearing its ugly head."

Phineas froze. He had never known Charlotte to hit so low or be so angry. "I knew you were mad at me. It didn't take much to bring it out."

He looked out the window, trying to calm himself by staring at the ocean waves that rolled onto shore, their rhythmic sound filling the silent room. When he left the kitchen and crossed to the family room, Charlotte followed, sitting beside him on the couch.

"I'm sorry. I didn't mean that you were demonic," Charlotte said quietly. "I'm just feeling helpless over Samantha. We made a mistake. We." Charlotte emphasized the last word.

He held his arms open to her and when she went to him, he held her close and stroked her hair as he had done so many times before in better circumstances. "I knew better. I've lived longer. And like you said, I used to live with Raven." Just as suddenly as he had made contact with Charlotte, he broke it, standing up and pacing in front of her. "Maybe her treachery has rubbed off on me."

Charlotte walked over to stand behind him. Craving the contact once more, she wrapped her lithe arms around his waist and rested her head on his back. Together they stood, not needing to say a word for enough had already been spoken.

Finally, Phineas turned around to face her. "I love you. And we're going to need each other's support to get through this. I've got your back."

"And I yours," she replied.

He turned and cupped her chin in his hands, looking at her with grave seriousness. "Charlotte, when we're safely back home...and I don't mean if...I mean when...we need to have a serious talk about our future."

"What do you mean?"

"Shadow," he said simply. "I know you want to see her when we go to the Romani Realms."

The name brought a smile to Charlotte's lips. "Not just in the Romani Realms. I can't wait for her to arrive here...as our baby."

"Charlotte, she's half demon, too. You met a small girl who seemed helpless, but you also witnessed her powers. What happens if those powers develop and manifest into what Raven was capable of?"

"She'll be our daughter. That won't happen. We'll teach her and love her and..."

"We can't risk it, Charlotte. We just can't."

As he spoke, Charlotte shook her head willing the unwanted thoughts to leave as readily as the tears that flowed freely from her eyes.

# # #

Unlike Charlotte, whose reaction to the news of their upcoming trip into the Realms resulted in worry and strife, Suki accepted the inevitable and was going to make the most of this last night at home. Maybe her calm demeanor was due to the fact that she had lived for centuries already. Perhaps it was because sitting across from her was James, who looked more appealing than a hot fudge sundae. Her mind could easily wander into the territory of negative thoughts, those that filled her with worry over her friends' survival and well-being. But, she was old enough to know that fate's hand would shake your life as it sees fit and she couldn't do anything about it.

"Whatcha reading?" She watched James appreciatively as he stretched out on the couch, obviously trying to get his mind off of tomorrow as well.

He looked up and when he saw that Suki was wearing only a peignoir of the sheerest silk, he cocked his head and raised an eyebrow. Tossing the magazine aside, his answer was immediate. "Absolutely nothing."

She approached where he lay on the couch and stood in front of him, tempting him. "You sure? Because I wouldn't want to distract you."

Suki made a show of turning to leave. "You seem busy. Maybe I should just head back into the..."

But James grabbed her by the wrist and pulled her down on top of him before the ridiculous thought could leave her mouth. "No you don't."

She giggled as his beard tickled her throat, throwing her head back to encourage his mouth to explore her neck. He readily obliged her silent request, moving his mouth tantalizingly over her pale skin. "James? You sure this isn't too much to ask? I do know how much you love that Wired magazine. All those gadgets and gizmos...I'd be hard pressed to find anything that would take over your interest."

He gently pushed down the thin strap of her negligee, kissing her collar bone and shoulder as it lowered. "I can think of one thing that might pique my interest." His hand cupped her breast, and as it moved to the other, he added, "...or two."

"Oh James," she sighed.

"Let's make the most of our last night." He lifted her into his arms and headed toward their room. Carrying her was no effort. He was strong and his desire for her even stronger.

# # #

Suki woke first, the early light creeping through the blinds and the sound of sparrows chirping the sun's arrival. She looked at James who still slept soundly, his chest rising and falling in delectable waves. She could stare at him for hours and still be enthralled with his masculinity and handsome features, but last night she was more enamored with his character. He knew her like no other and had a way of calming her even in the wake of a fateful day. Last night James was gentile when it suited him and then, as quickly as the wind changing course, he turned devilishly sexy.

As much as she hated to leave his side, she didn't want to risk James not getting as much rest as possible. She snuck from the bed to take a shower, giving him the quiet and space that each needed to be in top form for what lie ahead.

# # #

Chapter Forty-Three

R aven looked to Daniel with disbelief. "What did you say?" It was the kind of question that one asked when they didn't really want an answer.

"Samantha," he repeated.

"I heard you, but why? How could you possibly know that she is the new arrival? You're human. You don't have powers; you're just a man." Stating the obvious, the realization dawned. "Oh no. You don't still...not after we just..." Tears fell from Raven's eyes.

Daniel moved toward her, but she turned her back. "Please don't," she said. "Just tell me how you know."

"I don't know. Maybe I'm wrong."

But Raven shook her head because she sensed the truth as well.

"Maybe..." Daniel grasped for an answer, but none sufficient would come to mind. "Shit. Raven, I don't know how or why. I just do."

"It's this place. This fucking place!" She paced the room and then flipped on the television and tuned to the one news station that was broadcast in the Realms. The news was always biased, but in this case, there could be no distortion of the truth.

Daniel turned his attention to the television as well and when Samantha's image was shown, his expression registered shock. He never thought he would see her again, yet there she stood in the meadow, a mere hour's distance from his home. His face revealed awe and it was no wonder. She looked absolutely breathtaking, like the television star that the Realms had created. And while his emotion showed momentary happiness, he readily recovered as Raven eyed him critically.

"You see?" she said.

"What?"

"The way you look at her. You still love her."

"We've been through this. Doesn't what just transpired between us mean anything?"

"I should be asking you that same question. Honestly Daniel, you should have seen your face when she first appeared up there." She pointed to his television that hung high in a corner where the wall and ceiling met.

"It's nothing but surprise that you see on my face. If you want honesty, I can say without any hesitation that I wished she hadn't come back."

Raven nodded, knowing that Daniel spoke the truth, but it did little to ease her troubled mind. Samantha's life would be in demand by every fraction in the Romani Realms. The high officials would be impressed that she survived one trip into the Realms only to willingly come back for more. They would certainly take this as proof of her ability to instigate the Triad and control the powers of the greatest minds from Suki's past Releasors.

This wouldn't interest the soulless ones, however. They would only see Samantha's return as evidence of her strong will. They would want to keep her alive. Or, at least somewhat alive, more like a degree of complacent existence in which her strength of character could feed them for years to come.

Raven knew that Daniel would never want to see her go through any of this. As much as Raven hated the idea of helping Samantha, the best way to keep her man was to do just that, along with getting that girl out of here in one piece.

# # #

Chapter Forty-Four

S amantha no longer found herself in the midst of the ballroom. Without her leaving or any passage of time, the room transformed into a stage in which Samantha was the star. Standing center stage, she felt alone and exposed. The only thing she could be thankful for was that the annoying strobe light had ceased to blink. The room was quiet, eerie. It wasn't like the officials to be complacent and she suspected this time of reflection was fleeting.

In the meantime, she waited. Pacing back and forth like a bored lioness. The room became stuffy. Or perhaps, it only appeared to grow warmer, a symptom of the claustrophobic nature of her existence there. She lay on the floor, curled up in a ball with her head resting on her arm and fell asleep, not able to fight the demands of the trip any longer.

She awoke to a rhythmic drumming in what seemed like only minutes, but was in actuality well over an hour. The beating was everywhere and nowhere, all at once sounding as if it came from speakers around the room and then only within her own ears. It was typical of the Romani Realms environment to make one thing seem like another.

Samantha slowly pulled herself up to a seated position.

She held her head and rocked back and forth, but as she moved, the sound seemed to be louder below ground so she stood and paced. Pacing back and forth with nowhere to go and no plan of what to do.

A hidden voice boomed. "Welcome to confusion! Captivity does not appeal to innocents." And just like that, the drumming stopped.

Samantha also stopped pacing, realizing that they were mocking her. She looked out from the stage, trying to see if anyone were there, but she was met with further silence and solitude.

"What do you want? You cowards, just show yourselves!"

"Very interesting." The voice was amused. "You move through the set of emotions at a rapid pace for a human. One minute stuck inside confusion only to give way to the second emotion with hardly any battle."

"Shut up," Samantha screamed. "What are you talking about? What's this emotion that's so fascinating to you?"

"Anger!" The voice announced. "The second of prominent emotions. Our biology studies have concluded that this is indeed a natural progression following confusion. First confusion, followed by anger, giving way to lust and finally, resolve. Please observe further...for your viewing pleasure."

"F-You! I am not something to be observed. I will have you know that I intend to be a resident of the Romani Realms so I suggest you get used to me. I'm not going anywhere."

"In that case, perhaps you would enjoy this educational film? Are you sure you want to pass?"

"Yes! I mean, no, I don't!"

"Very well. We'll proceed," the voice said with a certainty that Samantha found disconcerting. "Your ambivalence makes for better viewing for our residents. We were only going to show you what was to come in order to level the playing field, so to speak. It's much more fun for us when you don't know what's coming."

With that declaration, a door slammed somewhere in the distance and footsteps could be heard approaching. The theater lights no sooner were dimmed and Samantha found herself waiting and wondering if she would regret her outburst.

Her anger waned giving way to apprehension when she saw a man's silhouette approach. As he neared and her eyes adjusted to the dim lighting, relief flooded through her when she saw Daniel's image.

She suddenly felt more in control, without realizing that she was again playing into the tricks of the Romani Realms. With every pace that Daniel took toward her, emotions grew stronger and the third of the prominent emotions indeed struck. Lust.

# # #

Chapter Forty-Five

T he quartet gathered at James' bar nervously
awaiting their trip into the Romani Realms.
There had never been a time when so many had
attempted to re-enter another realm simultaneously.

"Are you sure we shouldn't gather at the grave
site? After all, that is where Samantha found her path
into the Romani Realms, not once, but twice,"
Phineas pointed out.

"And, I followed her from the cemetery,"
Charlotte reminded the group.

James shook his head. "No, I'm adamant that it
has to be here. It's the only way I will have any control
over the paths we take."

"But James, we know where we'll land if we leave
from Samantha's old headstone." Charlotte's
expression revealed her elevated nerves.

James placed a comforting hand on her shoulder.
"I know this is hard for you. You're a strong person, a
loyal friend, and you've got a good head on your
shoulders. But Charlotte, when it comes to going with
the flow, you're a bit type-A. Just focus and trust."

Phineas released a small outburst of air that
spoke volumes. "Charlotte's not type-A," he said

sarcastically. "Are you sweetie? But as a demon gypsy, who is utterly devoted to you...I'm not going to let you out of my sight...or my control." He pulled her in for a hug to which she playfully punched his arm.

"I'm just feeling a bit insecure. I'm the only one of this group that's human and I'm not used to leaving my entire existence and life in other people's hands."

Suki had remained silent up to this point. Her Southern upbringing had taught her never to argue with her man in public. But it wasn't decorum that made her agree with James. It was his experience and the fact that he had always lived up to his duties as her Shade. He had protected her throughout time, even when she wasn't aware of his presence. Now that she knew he was behind the scenes for so many decades, even centuries, she thought of all the times that her outcome and destiny could have gone horribly wrong had it not been for James. He was loyal to her and she to him, and for that reason, she spoke her mind now freely.

"Charlotte, you don't have to feel helpless or less powerful than the rest of us. You're forgetting that you and Samantha were chosen to release me last year. That means you are special. Your didactic memory will be needed. You also know every historical fact from every one of my past Releasors. We're counting on you, too."

Charlotte bowed her head, embarrassed over Suki's compliment. "Thanks, Suki. I'll do my best."

"Speaking of which," James spoke up. "You're going to have to do just that right now. We each have a role to play, and yours Charlotte, is to tell us everything you've ever learned from Suki's Releasors who were involved in Plan 28."

Charlotte didn't waste a minute to prove her value. "Charles Babbage died in 1871. He was what's known as a polymath, a true Renaissance man. He was a mathematician, philosopher, inventor, and mechanical engineer."

"But, he was best remembered for originating the concept of a programmable computer. Betcha didn't know that I knew that." Phineas wagged his finger at Charlotte and gave her a flirtatious lift of his eyebrows.

"You wouldn't be standing there if I didn't recognize how smart you are." Charlotte began to relax in spite of the gravity of the situation in front of them. She kissed Phineas on the cheek. "And I'm glad you're here."

"I hate to break up your love fest, but..." James waved his palm upwards, the universal sign that indicated she should continue.

"Of course," Charlotte obliged. "Well, Babbage was also considered the father of the computer and credited with inventing the first one. But he also created a number of mechanical computers that weren't finished and those are on display in the London Science Museum. In 1991, some engineers studied Babbage's plans and created a perfectly functioning difference engine."

"Which is..." Suki asked.

"In the simplest of terms, it's a machine that calculates polynomial functions. Basically, calculating the variables of a particular equation. He didn't like to leave things to chance. If this new machine had been developed, it would be proof that Babbage could access and refine variables for a controlled result."

"Plan 28." James prompted Charlotte.

"Yes. Plan 28 was Babbage's idea for making time travel accessible."

"Accessible to...humans?" Suki uttered the last word as if she were afraid of what it could lead to.

"Yes." Charlotte smiled, now realizing that her gift was indeed a power. "If people were privy to Babbage's plans...specifically Plan 28...you wouldn't need to be a Shade, Genie, nor Demon Gypsy to leverage it." As she spoke each of the titles, she looked from James to Suki and let her eyes come to rest on Phineas.

"Just how much would something like that cost to make?" Phineas asked.

"You ready for it?" Charlotte asked, teasing her rapt audience. "In 2011, British researchers launched a multimillion-pound project to construct Babbage's Analytical Engine."

Phineas looked dubious. "What research facility has that kind of money for something as untested and for that matter, doubted in its existence as time travel?"

"Good question. Since Babbage's plans were continually being refined and were never completed, they plan to use crowd-sourcing to engage the public, leverage funds, and determine what aspects of the plan should be built."

"It's the ultimate memorial to Babbage," Suki said in awe.

"What do you mean?" Phineas spoke first.

"From what Charlotte says, Babbage believed in harnessing human mind skills to create advanced computing. Crowdsourcing is similar to human-based computation, which places humans and computers together to solve problems."

Charlotte nodded, pleased that Suki made the connection. "Suki, you're right on the money. But here's the kicker..." she paused, making sure that her audience was following along.

James, Phineas and Suki barely breathed, waiting for the next piece of the puzzle.

Charlotte continued, "Rather than a human telling a computer what to do as is the way we currently program, Plan 28 would utilize the computer's innate programable strength. In other words, the computer asks a person or in this crowdsourcing situation, a large group of people, to solve a problem. Then it collects, interprets, and integrates their solutions. The machine performs its function by outsourcing certain steps to humans. Not the other way around."

"It's genius," James applauded. "One tells the computer what it doesn't know how to do and let's the machine figure it out."

Charlotte tapped a finger to the end of her nose. "Bingo. And, this plan would have the equivalent of 675 bytes of memory, and run at a clock speed of about 7 Hz. Those who are involved hope to complete it by the 150th anniversary of Babbage's death, in 2021."

James spoke up, his dry wit evident. "We can't wait that long." Turning to Phineas, he added, "You and I both have experience from the Industrial

Revolution. The mirror will harness the steam power and will force the gears into motion. I need you to focus on controlling the souls that are trapped and don't let them interfere with Charlotte's thoughts. She has to be strong in order to get Plan 28 into effect."

"You got it." Phineas' normally jovial and joking mannerism changed to a serious tone.

"Good, that's covered," James continued before turning to his girl. "Suki...Charlotte will need your power as a guide. You are her muse and she'll need your calming affect in order to keep hers. Phineas will control the souls to keep them from talking to Charlotte, but he'll need help as well. You'll have to use the strength of your mind to calm Charlotte while also enabling Phineas to keep his mind on our mission...without worrying about Charlotte."

"Wait a minute, James...you said that I was supposed to keep the trapped souls from bothering Charlotte. Doesn't that mean I need to focus on her?"

James put an immediate stop to Phineas' disapproval. "I know what you're thinking, Phin, but it has to be this way. Focusing on the souls does not mean focusing on Charlotte. You have to be their bait. You cannot protect Charlotte during the trip. We need you to help harness the power of the machine. You have to trust Suki to look out for her."

Phineas looked to Suki. Knowing how much she had devoted herself to Samantha and Charlotte, he nodded his head once in full agreement.

"It's settled. We each have a job to do." James held out his left hand to Suki and his right to Charlotte, who then took Phineas', and connected to

Suki. The circle was formed. James spoke in a quiet, but strong voice.

"This won't be like last time. The four of us must be completely connected in thought in order for us to travel and land together. Wavering thoughts or emotions will cause one or all of us to lose our connection to each other. If you think of your future, your fears, even Samantha, it won't work. The only thought that can be on our mind is Plan 28."

Chapter Forty-Six

R aven moved about the cottage with nervous energy. She would try to sit and watch television, but the only viewing available were programs created by and for residents of the Romani Realms and presently, the only topic of interest was Samantha's arrival. As soon as Raven flipped the television on, she would immediately shut it down once again.

The cottage was cleaner than she had ever seen it. She even took a toothbrush to get into the small nooks where the floorboards met the walls. There was nothing else to do, unless she were to tend to the farm, but she didn't have Daniel's way with the equipment and tended to cause more harm than good where the crops were concerned. She didn't dare mess about with his livelihood right now, not when she feared that their entire relationship was on tender hooks.

She stared at the oversized, round clock that hung on the kitchen wall. The quiet ticking assured her that it was working even though the hands with delicate arrows that clicked at fifteen minute intervals seemed to have slowed their speed. It had been half an hour since Daniel left.

She knew the trip to the Romani Realms' main amphitheater would take that long and he was probably arriving now. That knowledge made her stomach ache with nerves and her heart beat erratically, or so it felt. He would probably spend at least half an hour with Samantha and then another thirty minutes to return. How she would spend the next hour was a concept that seemed filled with impossibility. She could only sit and contemplate their conversation before he left.

# # #

"I'm going to make this right, Raven." Daniel's words implied that "right" meant for both Raven and Samantha. The task was going to be a juggle and as much as Raven trusted and admired him, she wasn't sure that he was adept at keeping two women happy, nor did she believe that it was even possible. "I will go to her, tell her that it's over and send her back."

Fat chance. Raven knew if Samantha had risked coming back to the Romani Realms, she wasn't going to leave easily as if this was a casual shopping trip. "You'll need my help."

"I can't ask you to do that. I know how you feel."

"Don't you trust me?" Raven contemplated all the ways that she could get rid of Samantha, but then took a deep breath and pushed the thoughts away as quickly as they came to her. She had turned over a new leaf and if she wanted a future with Daniel, she certainly couldn't obliterate his former lover.

"Of course I do, but to ask you to help her, is a bit...awkward."

"I'm not going to do anything...inappropriate. And I recognize what you probably are thinking..."

He raised his eyebrows with a 'I'm not stupid' sort of expression. "Drowning her in the marsh or sending her to the Buraqs would not be very helpful. She's come back for a reason and I need to find out what it is."

Raven smiled, thinking to herself that men can be so naive. The reason was obvious, at least to her. "Daniel, you have experience here, but I have powers. If I don't help and something happens to her, then I'll be dealing with her mourning ex-boyfriend for the rest of time."

She took his hand. "I want you to be mine. But I don't want to risk that you'll live the present with me only to think about your past with her."

"Raven, I appreciate what you're saying, but I need to do this alone. I need to say goodbye once and for all. When she left last time she didn't want to leave and I didn't want her to either."

"That's just beautiful. Lovely. So happy to hear it. Good to know where I stand."

Arrival in the Romani Realms always affected one's ability to contain their emotions, but Raven couldn't blame that side effect since she had now been here for months. Still, a tear sprung to her eye and she huffed aloud and shook her head, showing that her new feelings for Daniel were real. She was amazed with the truth that love was stronger than any of her own powers.

Daniel smiled at her gently. "You okay?"

She nodded without speaking.

"Raven? Darling?" he was so bold to say, "I didn't finish my thought. Now, things are different. Samantha needs to know that."

Her eyes lowered and a smile graced her lips. She wanted to do a happy dance, but realized that would be poor form. Instead, Raven nodded, understanding the need for closure because she wanted it herself with Phineas. She had said and done so many ugly acts in the past. Being with Daniel made her want to be a better person, and right the wrongs.

She gave him a gentle kiss on the cheek. "I understand, but hurry back."

"I will. Lock the doors and hide under the floorboards if you hear anyone coming."

He did her one better. Brushing Raven's cheek with his hand, he said, "Do you mind if my kiss isn't merely for your cheek?" Before waiting for her answer, he kissed that cheek, let his lips grace closer and closer to her mouth, until he showed her how much he cared with a kiss to the lips that held a million promises.

# # #

Chapter Forty-Seven

T he mind games and voices of the Romani Realms were immediately forgotten. Upon seeing Daniel, Samantha rushed to him, throwing her arms around his neck without care as to who may be watching.

Daniel made the long trek to the theater with his mission clear. He would tell Samantha about his life, specifically that he had found love again. He didn't expect it to be an easy conversation. There was even doubt in his mind as to the wiseness of his timing, knowing that people's emotions were heightened from the journey. Still, this wasn't something he wanted to put off. He was determined not to lead her on and to send her back to safety as soon as possible.

But when Samantha ran to him, her beautiful mane of red hair flying behind her. Her eyes showed her love and shined with excitement. When she threw herself against him, his hands instinctively went to her waist and as she bounded against him, he picked her up and did a small twirl, not settling her onto the ground until they made a complete circle.

Just one circle of movement, a seemingly innocent response to her greeting. But in that moment it seemed his mind returned to her. Whether his heart would follow was still to be seen.

"You look beautiful." The words came out of his mouth, although he least expected them to.

She sighed aloud, her relief and pleasure on display. Then, in typical fashion of Samantha's exuberance and zest for life, she placed her hands on either side of his head and pulled him toward her. The kiss may have been initiated by Samantha, but it was returned by Daniel.

Without being able to stop himself, he gave into her demands, letting her lips cover his. The kiss may have gone on longer, but the voice from the loudspeaker boomed an interruption.

"Lust!"

The moment was immediately broken as Samantha was the first to realize the significance of the word beyond its definition. "The third pendulum of our emotions."

"What?" Daniel looked at her without comprehension.

"They're watching."

With that simple declaration, Daniel's face turned white. He knew better than to be surprised, after all, the officials saw everything. What worried him was not the fact that they had played with his emotions, as he now recovered himself and was reminded of the task at hand. He had not come here to continue his relationship with Samantha. The converse was true. But now, he worried what the officials were broadcasting and whether Raven also watched.

He backed away to the far end of the room, his hands on his hips, his brow furrowed with anger.

"Daniel? It's okay. I don't mind what they see." Samantha approached him in the darkened corner where he stood. "Let everyone know. It's why I'm here."

He turned to face her and as she reached to cup his cheeks, he grabbed her hands and held them to her sides forcibly. "No Samantha. I'm sorry. You have the wrong idea. Things cannot go back to the way they were."

She looked confused at first and then broke out into a laugh. "You are funny. I know you want me." She met his gaze seductively and then as if to prove a point, let her eyes lower to where proof of his desire still showed.

Daniel released his hold on her hands and held his own hands up, taking a step backwards to which Samantha only closed the gap between them once more. She wasn't the timid girl he had met earlier. Finding love and then returning for it made a woman out of her and she wasn't afraid to show him what she wanted. With no modesty, she placed her hand on the crotch of his pants, allowing her fingers to gently massage him.

"Samantha..." His voice was a warning.

"It's dark here. They can't see."

"That doesn't matter to me. I don't want..."

"Good," she interrupted. "It doesn't matter to me either." She didn't wait for any more excuses. Keeping her hand in place, she kissed him again and was pleased that his reaction became more defined. His mind may have not been on board, but his body was.

His hands groped at her back, pulling her in closer, feeding the need that grew.

"That's better," she murmured against his cheek as his lips ran along her cheek. Then, to her surprise, his tongue ran down her neck and moved toward her full breast that his hand had exposed. Roughly, he cupped her breast and let his mouth take her nipple. Hands and mouth seemed to move at a frenzied pace, covering her body all at once.

"Stop!" she whispered against his mouth. But his hands were reaching under her skirt, pulling at her panties. There was no stopping him. He moved like a man possessed.

Samantha whimpered, "Please...this isn't how I remember you."

He stopped for the briefest of moments, only to meet her gaze and his eyes turned red and his face shifted momentarily into the horse head of one of the Buraqs. Samantha screamed and the voice on the loudspeaker shouted, "Enough!"

She ran to the other side of the room when the Buraq released its hold on her. "Daniel?" She called to him, but no answer came. How he had transformed or whether he had ever been with her was unknown.

"What do you want?" she shouted at the now empty room as the Buraq had also disappeared.

"Resolve," the loudspeaker voice announced. "You will live as we tell you to...here forever."

# # #

Chapter Forty-Eight

S hadow was waiting. For a child, she was incredibly patient. Perhaps because as a demon, she knew she had all the time in the world. When the earth shook as it did when new arrivals landed, she clapped her hands with glee and ran to the community swing set. She liked to pump her little legs as hard as they would take her, elevating the swing to full height so that she could see her surroundings. She didn't want to be late.

The foursome had landed.

"Oh bother." She pushed the bodies of the hanging children aside each time their small frames interfered with her swinging. Invariably, one would hit her on the side of her head as the swing rose high to the top of the frame. "How am I supposed to see the good stuff?" she muttered aloud, pushing a hanging boy of about seven out of her way without any repulsion whatsoever.

As soon as she pushed one body, it would hit another. A hideous cat's cradle resulted with the dead children's hanging bodies slamming into one another and throughout it all, Shadow merely focused on catching sight of Charlotte, the one she was most anxious to see.

"Go away!" she shouted at the dead boy again. Finally, she gave up being able to see any details of the foursome's arrival and decided she would have to get closer.

Jumping off the swing set, she landed easily although her shoe plunged into a spot of mud. She bent and brushed off the patent leather school girl shoes, a throwback to a bygone era, and satisfied that they looked presentable, she wiped her hands on the grass and went forth to find Charlotte.

As she crossed the meadow, she tested out her practiced greeting. "Miss Charlotte. No," she shook her head. "Mommy. Mom. Mother?"

Shadow let the choices play over her tongue, and finally decided on Mommy because she had always wanted one and knew that the moniker would likely please Charlotte as well. She nodded once to herself, took a deep breath and carried on down the path that would lead her past the meadow and toward the forest.

# # #

Chapter Forty-Nine

S amantha balled up her fists in frustration as tears welled in her eyes. The fact that she was reduced to a sniveling school girl when she had moments earlier felt like a woman wasn't lost on her. She knew their game, but she was damned determined not to play it. "I may decide to live here, but it will be my choice. You will not see me following your orders. Never!" As if to emphasize her point and the futility of it, she stomped her foot upon the last exclamation.

The sound of many pairs of hands clapping ensued. Initially, just a single one and then shortly afterward, a plethora of applause swallowed her up. The sound went on and on until Samantha became noticeably uncomfortable. The spotlight that had shone down on her previously returned when her resolve did. Simultaneously, the applause died down so the voice could be heard.

"The phase of Resolve shall begin. You may leave."

Initially, Samantha didn't move, unsure of what to do or where to go. It wasn't until the lights around the theater returned, the heavy curtains over the floor-to-ceiling length windows were lifted and a single door opened that she allowed her feet to move from their spot. The outside sunshine hit her face with pleasant warmth compared to the frigid air-conditioning of the theater. A gently breeze brushed her hair from her face. If she weren't so aware of the dangers and evils that lurked, this place might seem idyllic.

Tentatively, she turned toward her right, holding her breath for she knew the swing set would soon appear in her sights. She exhaled with relief upon seeing it empty. Not a child, living or otherwise, was present although the swings gently rotated in the breeze.

Samantha took a moment to stand still to check her bearings and figure out her next move. She remembered that in order to reach Daniel's house she must travel through the forest, although the idea of going there alone, even if it meant seeing Daniel again, was not something she relished.

As the wind picked up, blowing the swings even harder and causing them to release an eerie creaking sound, a single crow descended and landed on the nearest one. Samantha eyed it warily, wondering if it could be Raven although it appeared too small to be so.

It cawed angrily at her and immediately others filled the sky and landed on the swings. They took up every imaginable space, not only with their bodies but also the sound of their caws, which seemed to mock her until Samantha took off toward the forest at a run.

# # #

Daniel didn't mind the forest, but being deposited in the midst of it was disconcerting. There was no time to assess who was about, nor could he mentally prepare himself for the journey. Moving past the stretching hands of the soulless ones as they protruded from the murky mud, he listened carefully for any footsteps beyond his own.

He would be lying to not admit that seeing Samantha had more of an effect on him than he wanted. Was he a coward to have not told Samantha about Raven or because he felt relieved at being catapulted away from her without warning? While debating this quandary in his mind, he picked up the pace when heavy footfalls echoed behind him.

Within a few moments, two Buraqs joined him, one on either side. They observed his deliberate gait and when Daniel didn't slow or even acknowledge their presence, their horse heads whinnied to him. Still he ignored them.

The one on his left shoved his shoulder against Daniel, but he merely continued his pace. The Buraqs nakedness were disturbing to most men particularly since they were strong beasts, but Daniel had years of experience in the Romani Realms. He had learned that focusing the mind was essential. He would not be deterred.

The second moved in front to block his path. When Daniel was forced to halt, the creature addressed him in perfect English. "Where are you going? You know that you have to address us. Bow down."

Daniel would gladly fight both of the creatures rather than lead them to Raven. But to do so could have a debatable outcome. Weighing up the pros and cons of irritating them in the forest where other evils resided or deal with them on his home turf, Daniel decided he had no choice but to escalate the situation and deal with it immediately.

Buraqs lived for trepidation. They thrived on fear. He would show them neither. "I'll be on my way and there won't be any trouble." Daniel's voice was even and he met their sideways glances head on.

The Buraqs laughed and began to close in on him, each shoving their strong bodies against his. They stood at least five inches taller than Daniel, but his hours of farming gave him an edge when it came to upper body strength. Their lower bodies, however, were muscled sinew from hours of running for the Romani Realms officials. Their only duty was to patrol and intimidate and as they stood close with their manhood on display, the effectiveness of their skills became evident.

"This one thinks he doesn't need to go down on his knees for us." As the Buraq spoke, his manhood protruded obscenely. Daniel turned away, disgusted at his show. It was his first mistake.

"I told you to kneel. Show respect for your Buraqs who uphold the rules of the Romani Realms."

Daniel knew that shielding his eyes from them would only serve to give them power. They had no shame, no modesty. He had to show them that it didn't affect him or risk them following and taunting him all the way to his homestead. "I do not follow the government of the Realms. I am granted independent immunity."

"Impossible!" shouted the lead Buraq. "Immunity is only for those who reside here voluntarily and no sane person does that."

"I do."

The Buraq squinted its horse eyes at Daniel before speaking again. "Second, immunity is for those who have their own means of livelihood and do not rely on the government for resources."

Once again, Daniel spoke the clear phrase that made the Buraqs question their own authority. "I do."

"And what do you do?"

"I am a farmer."

"And you grow...?"

"Everything. I grow everything I need. And since I have no need for you, let me pass."

The Buraq shook his head, although more tentatively than before. "Third. Immunity is only for those who can successfully pass the Buraq forces and that certainly isn't you..."

A new resident of the Romani Realms might be caught by surprise, but Daniel had experience on his side. Without a moment's hesitation, he sent a roundhouse kick to the side of the Buraq's head. They didn't have a chance to get in the first attack. Daniel's offense was swift and efficient with another kick to the first and his knee to the groin of the second.

He fought with determination, never stopping. Daniel focused on attacking them straight on, landing kick after kick and using their peripheral vision as a weakness until it was over.

With both Buraqs down, he facilitated one final shove – his boot against the leader's jaw in a show of strength. With immense calm, he spoke, "I'll be on my way now."

# # #

Chapter Fifty

R aven was desperate for Daniel to come home as the waiting was killing her. She felt restless and with each passing minute the feeling intensified until it wasn't enough to pace, to clean, or even to walk the grounds. She needed to leave.

She scribbled a hurried note, ensuring Daniel that she was fine, but felt the need for some air. He would understand, she reasoned with herself. "It's just a walk."

But as she started down the path, she knew that there was something else bothering her. What started as worry and perhaps jealousy over the possibility of Daniel reconnecting to Samantha had taken a turn. Concern still flooded her mind, but it was mixed with an energy that she couldn't quite put her finger on. It was supernatural, a pull of some sort, but towards what she couldn't determine. That is, until the ground shook and an immediate flash of Phineas appeared in her mind.

"No. I'm over him!" She shouted the words skyward, needing the powers that controlled both of their emotions to listen. True, they would always share a connectedness, but that didn't have to mean anything beyond their shared past. But what she felt at the moment was an undeniable need that stirred deep in her core and filled her every thought. The good and bad of their relationship flipped like a fast shutter, showing her image after image of the two of them together until she was desperate to see him to determine what was going on within herself.

With purpose, she left the homestead she now shared with Daniel, taking one glance over her shoulder – a futile attempt to convince herself to stay.

# # #

The foursome landed in the meadow, each feeling the effects of the trip into the Romani Realms. Both Suki and Charlotte vomited; James merely sat with his head in his hands, seemingly trying to get his bearings. Only Phineas was able to walk around, but that in itself was part of his problem. Whereas the others were subdued and tired. He was wired, unable to sit still and immediately feeling his past connection to Raven that affected him like the strongest of aphrodisiacs. He kept his distance from Charlotte as he didn't trust his own tongue.

James eyed him uneasily knowing that the Realms had gotten to him. When he was finally able to pull himself to a standing position, he walked over to Phineas.

"You are so fucking jittery. Get a hold of yourself," James chastised.

"I'm good."

"Like hell."

Phineas indicated where Charlotte and Suki sat about one hundred yards away. "Just be cool. I don't want Charlotte to know what's up."

"Well, what is up?"

"Raven...the lust pull."

James looked both repulsed and curious all at once. "What is that?"

"It's like a porno playing in my mind. I see and feel every moment of our past, but it's all condensed. Like your memories on speed."

James placed his hands on his knees and leaned over as if the very thought of what Phineas was going through was too much for him to stomach. "Oh man, that sounds...I mean, Raven is intense in small doses. I can't even imagine what you're going through. How long were you together? Like centuries?"

Phineas nodded, his eyes closing as if to ward off the thought.

James patted him on the back. "It'll pass."

"That's your advice? Excellent. Really good." Phineas shook his head with disbelief. "You don't have anything better for me?"

"Well, you said it yourself. It's like a drug. So, go cold turkey. Mind over matter. Just don't think about it. Be strong."

Phineas looked over to where Charlotte was now pulling herself up to a standing position and appeared to contemplate making the walk over to where the two men stood. "You know what, James? For a bartender, I would have thought you could come up with much better advice."

"Okay, how 'bout this? Just bat those baby blues at Charlotte and I'm sure she'll take care of you.

Besides, there's no point in worrying about Raven right now. You don't even know where she's located."

The words had barely left James' mouth when a large crow swooped down low and grazed the top of Suki's head. "Hey!" she said, struggling to stand up in order to not be a target.

Suki rose just as the crow spread its wings wide and landed in front of them, changing into the form of Raven as it did.

# # #

Chapter Fifty-One

S amantha's brisk stride was helping to improve her mood. She was making good time over the steep grade from the forest lowlands into the mountain region where Daniel lived. She would have run there if able, but the combination of the altitude as well as not wanting to attract more unwanted attention forced her to maintain a modest pace.

In truth, she didn't know if she would even find Daniel at home when she arrived. For that matter, it wasn't clear in her head if Daniel had even been with her in the theater. It certainly seemed like him – initially. There was no point in feeling embarrassment over what had transpired in the theater. Either it was Daniel and he would understand that the sadistic officials were having their fun, or he hadn't even been present and therefore, Samantha had all the reason to return.

Either way, she was determined to convince him that they should be together. Just the two of them in a mountain retreat. The fact that the romantic hideaway that she envisioned in her imagination was perched above the Romani Realms didn't enter into the equation. If Daniel could be granted immunity from the evils of this place than certainly his wife could as well, which is what she had planned for her future. She would see to it.

When Samantha arrived and headed down the path that led behind Daniel's house to the acres of fields he tended, the sun was high in the sky. So bright in fact that he didn't immediately recognize her. He was wearing a wide-brimmed hat as he hoed new lines in the dirt and he smiled with relief and waved to her when he heard footsteps. Taking his expression as one of eagerness over her arrival, Samantha ran to him. It wasn't until she was nearly upon him that he shielded his eyes from the sun. Immediately, his smile vanished.

"What are you doing here?"

"That's not a proper way to greet me," she said and walked directly to his front door and into his house, calling over her shoulder, "I prefer the way you did it at the theater."

Daniel shoved the hoe into the dirt and reluctantly followed her. He wasn't altogether clear of what had happened at the theater, and hoped that Samantha also realized this truth. He was about to find out.

He didn't like seeing Samantha in his kitchen, making herself at home the way she used to. It felt wrong. This was no longer her domain. "I thought you were someone else. And, as for us in the theater, you have no idea what happened." His voice was stern. His tone distant.

But Samantha was intent on warming his cool demeanor. "It sounds to me as if you experienced something..." Her voice was flirtatious. "I'll tell you what I remember. We shared a kiss. And it was good."

Daniel looked noticeably uncomfortable with the news. He did indeed remember a kiss, but after experiencing it and being transported back to his home, he had hoped that it was only a trick of his mind and that Samantha hadn't actually been privy to it.

"I can't be with you, Samantha." Best say it fast and without any hesitation. Like ripping off a bandage, he believed without hesitancy was the best way.

"But we were in love. You said so."

Her expression pained him, but he carried on nonetheless. "I didn't expect to ever see you again. It hurt, but I moved on."

Hurt...the very word instilled it within herself. But the feeling vanished as Samantha was reminded of the taunting voice in the theater. Resolve. They wanted her to accept her fate. To live in the Romani Realms without hope or love or any goodness whatsoever. She shook her head, a testament that she would not give up.

She eyed Daniel, trying to see what he wasn't willing to show. "Why? Why would you not want me again? Unless..."

It didn't matter where a person came from or what they had experienced. People are basically cut from the same cloth and men even more so. Nary a man would turn away from a beautiful woman, unless another was in his heart.

"There's someone else," she said accusingly.

"That's true."

Samantha plopped herself down on Daniel's couch even though an invitation to stay hadn't been extended. She covered her eyes with her hands and rested her elbows on her knees. Staying in that hidden position, she tried to piece together what Daniel wasn't revealing.

"Maybe you're not the man I thought you were if you can just run off with the first pretty face."

"It's not like that."

Samantha softened as hope was extended. "So, it's not someone new. I knew it. It's the officials. You wouldn't just cast me aside." Samantha stood up and ran to Daniel, again throwing her arms around his neck. "We can figure this out. We'll be together again."

"No, Samantha." Daniel detangled himself from her hold. "You misunderstood me. I didn't 'go off with the first pretty face' as you say. It's someone I knew. Raven."

The name stung like a slap. "How could you? Of all people. She...she is the reason that I'm here. She sent me here."

"I know all that, but you don't really know her...and you don't know me. Raven and I...we're right for each other."

"How can you say that?" Tears flowed freely down her cheeks.

Daniel didn't want to justify his decision, but he didn't want to hurt Samantha. Being with her was never ideal. She wasn't meant to live in the Romani Realms. He needed her to understand that sending her back home may have been painful, but it was right.

"Samantha, did you ever think to ask why I'm here? Why I make this place my home and would rather make it livable than try to return outside of these Realms? You left the Realms. Don't you think I could too...if I wanted?"

Samantha looked down neither wanting to hear his words, nor willing to contemplate his answer.

"That makes no sense. Nobody stays here, if they don't have to. It's full of the dead...people who were never meant to be born...criminals."

"And the guilty."

She looked at him without understanding. When he motioned for her to sit down again, she did so without words.

"Samantha, I was married once. I was young when we got together, and pretty typical of a guy in that I wanted to play around, but my family was old-fashioned and felt getting married would force me to settle down and be more responsible. They wanted me to take over the family farm and have babies."

"What happened?"

Daniel looked up at the ceiling, crossing his arms behind his head and then resting it on the back of the couch. It had been a long time since he had contemplated everything that had happened. They weren't memories that he relished reliving.

"Like I said, my family was old-fashioned. We had a church wedding. I took over the responsibilities on the farm, which was located a good hour's drive from the nearest town and that consisted of only the necessities – a hardware store, grocery store, a school...and a bar. At first, we lived the way we were supposed to live – at least the way my parents had lived. We spent every waking moment together, from sunrise to sunset. I took care of the land; she took care of the animals. And at night, we worked on making a baby."

"Okay then." Samantha shifted uneasily on the couch. "So, what was the problem."

"Cancer was the problem." Daniel didn't mince words. "She got sick and the drive to the doctor was even farther than the town. Once a week, we drove two hours away for treatments. By the time we were finished, she was too tired to do anything but be in bed. I know it sounds selfish, but the emotional toil on me was hard. When I went into town alone to go to the hardware store or for groceries, I found myself stopping in at the bar 'for just one drink.'"

He made quote marks in the air as he said the last words, nodded to himself with the memory, and then settled back on the couch again before continuing his story.

"I was a mess."

Samantha leaned forward to touch his sleeve. "That's understandable. You must have been devastated to watch someone you love..."

"Don't pity me, Samantha." There was a hard edge to Daniel's voice and he moved his arm away from her touch. "The bartender was a woman who was young and vibrant. She wasn't even that pretty, but she wasn't needy. She didn't represent obligation or responsibility. One day, she handed me my drink, gave me the bill and when I had everything I needed, she asked me what I really needed."

Without being able to stop it, Samantha's right eyebrow rose with the implication of Daniel's words.

He turned to her, and acknowledged what she was thinking. "Yep, that's right. I just needed someone to have sex with. Someone who would give themselves to me without taking a thing in return. She was able to do that and even more so, she was willing to do so on a regular basis. So I started looking forward to my weekly visits into town and staying longer than necessary."

Samantha tried to process the information, her thoughts twisting with a desire to sympathize with his story, but mainly she hated to learn that he wasn't the man she believed him to be.

"Many people would understand the pressures you faced," she said cautiously, forcing herself to believe her own verbal lie. "You may have been justified. I'm sure you didn't carry on this affair for long."

"May have been? You're sure I didn't..." His voice rose, but he refused to finish or repeat the sentence. "Like I said, Samantha, you don't know me."

"I want to." She took his hand, but still he refused contact with her.

"My wife did get worse. She went into hospice care because I couldn't care for her alone. But even then, I continued to go into town. Nobody questioned it because the farm had to be maintained."

"Okay, so you did what you had to do."

"Stop it, Samantha! Stop trying to make me out to be some hero you imagine. Some wonderful guy who saved you from this place. I'm no such man. I was in the arms of my lover when my wife died alone!"

No further words were spoken. For an excruciating minute the two sat in stony silence.

Finally, Samantha couldn't remain quiet. Either curiosity or awkwardness forced her to ask the ultimate question. "But how did you end up here?"

"I couldn't bear the guilt. I contemplated killing myself, but I was raised that to do so was a sin and besides, it seemed like too easy of a way out. Why should I just be able to end it at will? So, I read everything I could about black magic. Sought out people who could help me and had my blood poisoned, but my body maintained. I took a cocktail of heroine and rat poison, flushed it through my system with an IV and then, when it appeared as if my heart and brain could take no more, they resurrected me.

The heroine served to transport me to the most hideous place my mind could imagine – here. And this is where I remained, even though my former body was returned to the earth."

"Was there a funeral?" Samantha asked quietly, wondering if it was indeed similar to how she had been resurrected.

"I assume so. Although, I don't think I had many attendees."

Samantha nodded to herself, taking in the information. "You could still change your mind," she said finally, as if after processing the news she had made her own decision about Daniel's guilt.

He stood up and stormed to the front door. "You're unbelievable. You haven't heard a word I've said. I don't have a magical genie looking out for me, like you do. I can't just come and go. I don't want to anyway. I want to live here, find a bit of peace, but most importantly, being here helps me remember what I've done. It's my penance."

Listening to his words had stirred a frenzy in Samantha. Tears now flowed freely and she coughed uncontrollably while making hiccuping noises. She ran to Daniel, throwing her arms around his waist and pressing her body against his. "Let me be the one to take your mind off the past. I don't care about it. I fell in love with you and I came back for you. That's what I'm going to do."

"I don't want you. Raven understands me better. She's better suited for me. If I ever change my mind, she has the power to help me. You can't do anything for me other than to remind me of humanity and what I did when I lived in that world. Your friends will be coming for you. I'm sure you'll figure it out." He opened the door. "Now go!"

"Isn't there anybody decent here?" She tentatively stepped out beyond the threshold.

"I made a choice, Samantha. I could have mourned my wife and then lived alone as the good, grieving widower. Would you want that man?"

She shrugged, but the motion only incensed Daniel further.

"You think Raven is so bad? What kind of woman are you to want someone who is telling you I turned my back on a dying woman who I had made vows to? I chose to end my own life out of cowardice. I couldn't live with the knowledge of my indiscretion and for the first time, I'm with someone who truly can understand my torment. It's obvious that you can't."

"That is not true! I would be better for you. I accept you. I don't care about the past. Raven...she's horrible." Samantha threw up her arms out of frustration. "How could you choose someone like her? Unless...it's just another way of punishing yourself. She's disgusting. So, if that's the reason, then bravo!"

He shook his head and really looked at Samantha, as if seeing her for the first time. "She's not." His voice was quiet and calm. "She understands – humanity. I know it sounds ironic, but it's true. She loved a man only to have him betray her. She lost her family. She was sick and alone and the one man who helped her was later stolen from her by her best friend...Suki. She thought she found love in Phineas, but realized that his allegiance to her wasn't as much about love as it was survival."

"And then she struck out at me!"

"I know."

The sun was beating down on them, but Daniel didn't make a move to ask her back inside the house. If anything, his glance down the walkway indicated that he wished she would leave soon in case Raven returned.

"I made a choice, Samantha."

"To die?" she sobbed. "You are the one decent person here. You don't belong here."

As if validating her statement, he softened and reached for her hand. In a softer voice, he said his final words. "I didn't say it was the right choice."

They stood for a moment in silence. His hand on hers, and Samantha desperately wanting it to stay there.

"Samantha, our choices of the past affect the future. Be careful when making your own decisions."

She threw her arms around him, only to have Daniel untangle himself from her embrace once again. She shook her head at him, willing his news to be undone, wanting him to take back the unwanted gesture. "Please don't," she whispered.

"Raven is not the person you think she is. She's experienced the gamut – love, betrayal, vengeance – the highs of power, the lows of being overthrown. She could have taken on any persona, but she has lived long enough to know what she wants...and I'm happy to say it's living a simple life with me. No more drama. No attempts at ultimate power. Just our love."

"Love?!" Samantha spat out the word.

"But I'm back. How can you say that?"

He looked her dead in the eye and said the words she never expected to hear from him. "You shouldn't have come back."

# # #

Chapter Fifty-Two

"**D**on't get too comfortable." Raven walked among the foursome, trying to appear aloof in spite of her feelings to the contrary. She needed them – more than she cared to admit.

The moment she transformed into human form, the crows that accompanied her left. Their mass exodus caused Charlotte to duck her head while Suki made a cringing expression.

"They're just birds," Raven chastised.

"More like rats with wings," Suki muttered.

"Nice to see you too, Suki." And then turning to Phineas, Raven added, "...and the rest of you."

Phineas gave her an awkward wave while Charlotte elbowed him in the ribs. "What? It's not like we can ignore her."

"No, you can't," Raven agreed. "You're going to need me. You're all going to need me," she said to Charlotte pointedly as she was the only one in the group with the most to lose by being in Raven's presence.

"I don't trust her," Charlotte whispered at barely an audible decibel.

Still, Raven heard her with supernatural clarity. "Please...as if I have an interest in her...or you for that matter, Phin." She rolled her eyes to which Phineas again smiled. "Maybe we should try to all get along," he suggested. "Raven, we're here to collect Samantha. Have you seen her?"

"Oh yeah, we were having tea earlier and later we're getting our nails done. Of course I've seen her!"

"So where is she?" Suki asked.

"Everywhere."

"What do you mean?" James moved forward.

"That girl has always been impetuous. Suki, I don't know how you put up with it. She needs to be reined in, like a horse. Maybe it comes from not growing up with a mother? But she has spirit, I'll give her that." Raven sighed, collecting her thoughts. "You'd think that sending her to the Realms last year would have done the trick, but no...she comes right back like a bad penny. How am I supposed to keep her safe?"

The others were gob-smacked at the flow of thoughts coming from Raven. They watched as she sat down on a clump of grass and plucked a daisy that grew nearby, casually pulling its leaves in a loves-me-loves-me-not fashion.

"She arrives here and immediately causes a stir. I guarantee there isn't a council member that doesn't know about her arrival. I tell you, I'm going to have a hell of a time distracting them. It's not like I'm their favorite right now. Nope. I've got a slew of my own problems and now, Samantha too."

The foursome stared at her, slightly baffled at the obvious change in her personality.

"Uhh, Raven? You seem kinda off your kilter." Suki sat down next to her and peered into her eyes, not so much as to make contact, but more to analyze Raven.

"Oh stop staring, Suki. You used to always do that when I was upset as if you could spot all the problems and poof, make them disappear. The only thing I need to disappear is that Releasor of yours."

Suki glanced up at James with wide eyes, showing him that she was as confused as anyone over Raven's openness. "Your turn," she stood up and indicated that James should take a crack at figuring out this side of Raven.

He took the cue and sat down, but immediately, Raven put up her hand in the stop motion. "Not so close. I've been having some...issues."

"Issues?" Suki asked.

"Seems my *experiences*," she emphasized the word, "with past lovers is affecting my sensibilities. So, when I'm with someone now, every once in awhile I start reliving what it was like with someone I was with in the past."

James inched himself backwards a foot. "Even me? It was only once."

Suki stamped her foot, hating the reminder. James immediately gave her the palms up signal that begged what-can-I-do?

"So far, so good with you," Raven admitted. "I'm probably safe from that memory. But Phin..." she looked over to him, "our pasts are much more entwined and it's been a bit problematic for me lately, to say the least."

"I know what you mean," he said without a second thought.

"What?!" Charlotte faced him, causing Phineas to close his eyes momentarily, hoping to avoid confrontation.

Knowing he was caught, he uttered the only word that seemed appropriate. "Shit."

"Yeah, it certainly is," Charlotte agreed.

Raven spoke up. "Grow up, Charlotte. I don't want him. It's just a pull of the Romani Realms."

Charlotte remained with her arms crossed. But Phineas, still reeling from the journey and unable to fully contain himself, blurted his thoughts. "The timing of those visions is crazy, huh?"

Raven blushed in spite of herself and locked eyes with Phineas who she had to admit still looked as delicious as ever.

"Phin, are you saying that you thought of *her* when you were with *me*?!"

"Not on purpose," he added quickly.

"Kids...can we move forward," Suki suggested. "Raven, what do we need to do to get Samantha home?"

Raven motioned for them to follow her. She sat down under the eaves of a large oak tree and the others followed, including Charlotte who trailed behind last. When they were all seated in a circle, Raven hit them with news that none expected.

"James...Suki...you know how to get out of here. And Phineas, your powers are strong enough to carry Charlotte back home. You just need to focus your minds, think only about your desire to get home, and leave everything else behind."

"By 'everything else' you mean all of our concerns and thoughts. You don't mean Samantha," Charlotte interjected, her distrust obvious.

"Of course not!" Raven's irritability matched Charlotte's. "But need I remind you that I've given you everything you could possibly want for a happy life. Phineas' bond to me is broken. Samantha is alive. I just want you all to leave this place and leave me alone. Just go."

"We can't leave without her," Charlotte added.

Raven stood up and dusted off her behind. "Then let's go get her."

"Wait," Suki called to her. "After everything? Why would you help us?"

Raven turned to face the group, her eyes narrowed, her chin pointing upward and proud. "Because if there's anyone who wants you out of here, it's me."

# # #

Chapter Fifty-Three

Determined that the conversation was over, Daniel tried to close his front door, but Samantha forced her body against it.

"You don't mean those things. Fear or something in this place has forced you to say those horrible words to me. You don't have to do this."

"Samantha, I'm doing this because I don't want you to be hurt, but sometimes the truth does hurt. However, I'd much rather my words sting than you stay here and succumb to the atrocities of the government. They will use your soul and feed the residents from it. We are not going to be together, so go home. Make a safe life for yourself."

Knowing she wouldn't leave unless forced to do so, he took her arm and led her down the path, walking her toward the edge of his property before pointing that she should continue.

He waited with hands on hips, unwavering in his decision. Finally, Samantha turned around and took off at a run, the sound of her sobs floating on the air. Daniel sat and placed his head in his hands, face held downward and his mood even lower. He never wanted to hurt her, but he no longer wanted to be with her.

His past wasn't right for Samantha's future. He couldn't be the man she thought he was. For that matter, he didn't want to be. He wanted to have his memories of what he had done wrong and he wanted a woman who wouldn't try to change him. Raven. With all his heart, he knew that Raven was the right woman for him.

He collected his thoughts and once again became at ease with his decision. The pleasant scent of lavender that grew wild masked the stench of oncoming trouble that blew in on the wind. The realization that something was awry came fast and unexpected. Horse hooves pounded in the distance, their clamoring echoing from the canyon below his cottage.

"Damn it!" Daniel took off at a run, hurrying to catch up to Samantha. Fortunately, she hadn't maintained her fast pace. He found her just barely a quarter down the path from his home, sitting and crying, lost in her sadness. When she heard him approach, she looked up with a tear-streaked face that was marred with the dirt of the path. Remnants of her hasty departure showing on her otherwise pale skin.

"Hurry!" he said, offering his hand.

"Where?"

Without wavering, Daniel answered, "Back to my place."

Her eyes widen in surprised confusion. "Why?"

"Because they're looking for you. They'll sacrifice you to the soulless ones before you even know what's happening."

# # #

To Raven's annoyance, Suki stopped walking. The sun was beating down and the others seemed thankful that she had the courage to do what they wanted.

"Listen, I know it's hot, but your lily white skin would much rather suffer a bit of a sunburn than deal with the consequences of us being late in finding Samantha," Raven barked.

"That's just it...Samantha's heart beat has quickened." Suki placed a hand on her own heart, trying to slow it while taking deep breaths.

Raven steadied her own nerves. "Are you sure? Maybe it's the altitude. Keep up already."

James took Suki's hands in his own, trying to steady her. "Talk to me."

She nodded and took a deep breath. "It's not the altitude. There's a threat to Samantha." Turning to Raven, she asked, "What can it be? Tell us every possibility."

Raven hesitated, not wanting to contemplate everything that could go wrong. If Samantha was caught here she knew that the pressure would be off of her. The soulless ones would have enough to feed on from her for years. Samantha's innocence would sustain them and the government would no longer have an interest in her own powers. But Daniel would certainly be changed. He was too good of a person to not have something like that affect him, and it would certainly affect their relationship. She knew her goal in helping Samantha may not be for completely pure reasons, but still, she would do her best to save her.

In a small voice, because she couldn't muster anything stronger, Raven spoke the truth. "It could be the Buraqs...or the soulless ones...either may have been sent to get her. I wouldn't have thought they would be a threat so early, but if Samantha attracted a lot of attention when she arrived, there may be no way to hold them off. Although, they usually like to toy with their prey for awhile...we may still have time."

James spoke to Suki again. "Could that be it? Is that what you see?"

Suki furrowed her brow in concentration. "It's odd," she admitted. "I felt her heart quicken and that's usually a sign of fear, but I don't see the soulless ones. I see what she sees; I feel what she feels."

"So what is it then?" Raven asked.

"What's making her heart beat a bit quicker is Daniel. He's walking with her and they're heading to his home. But Samantha looks...the only way I can describe it is like the cat who ate the canary."

Suki's expression showed bafflement, but Raven's was pure dread. The two women looked at each other, neither one expecting the reaction of the other.

# # #

Chapter Fifty-Four

Raven looked concerned, but she recovered her emotions quickly, masking them when Suki caught her eye.

"Suki, you haven't recovered from the journey. Your 'powers'..." she said using quotation fingers and mocking her longtime frenemy, "are impaired."

"How can you be so sure that my powers, which I'll have you know are perfectly intact, are misleading me? My instincts tell me that Samantha is with Daniel, which is why she came here. There's no reason to doubt it...and yet, you do. Why?"

Four pairs of eyes landed on Raven waiting for enlightenment.

"It's nothing. She means nothing to him." The answer only served to drum up more questions.

"What are you talking about?" Suki asked.

"Daniel...and me." Raven pressed her lips together and lowered her eyes as if she didn't want to reveal any more or have any other information extracted.

James, who had remained quiet thus far, spoke up. "You and Daniel? What is it about you and men? Can you possibly avoid seducing every man you come into contact with?"

"It's a curse," Raven said simply and kicked the ground as she moved slightly away from the group to

gather her thoughts. She didn't like the idea that
Samantha had gone back to Daniel's place. Yet, she
had fallen in love with his humanity and it was
probably that aspect of him that led to a cup of tea
before telling Samantha that he couldn't be with her.
At least she hoped.

As Raven paced, alone in her thoughts and trying
to push her own insecurities aside, the others stewed
in the new found knowledge of Raven and Daniel –
together.

"Well, I never thought the guy had it in him,"
Phineas muttered.

"You're telling me," James agreed with his friend.
"But you can imagine how it happened. This place,
her charms..."

"Her curves...," Phineas added.

"Those curves...," James agreed without thinking.

Suki elbowed him in the ribs while Charlotte gave
a less than gentle shove to Phineas' shoulder. "Hey!"
they exclaimed in unison.

James tried to back out of his faux pas, but only
buried himself deeper. "It's the Romani Realms...It's
not like I have total control of my thoughts."

Suki looked ashen. "So you still have thoughts
about her...those kind of thoughts?"

Phineas chose this inopportune time to come to
his friend's aid. "He can't help it. She's hot."

That's when Charlotte placed her hands on her
hips and turned to face her love. "You too?"

Phineas merely shook his head and shrugged his
shoulder. "Men look. It doesn't mean we touch."

"Hhmmpf," Suki snorted. "You've both already
done enough touching with that girl to last a lifetime."

"Excuse me!" Raven raised her voice and the quartet turned to face her, having completely forgotten that she was even among them. The grouping was so alien to all of them. "Can we get going? If you're all finished discussing my charms, that is?"

Suki nodded her agreement before chiming in. "Yes, let's get moving. I see now why you want us to leave so desperately. Well, it's time to get your *boyfriend*...God, I can't believe I'm even saying that...get you two back together. And then, then we can leave this place and the memories behind."

Raven met Suki's eye and a moment passed between them. The years of friendship, followed by even more years of hatred circled their minds. They had been through everything together but one thing remained true – time heals. And with that knowledge, both seemed to want to put the past behind them and move on with their rightful lives.

# # #

Chapter Fifty-Five

D aniel hurried Samantha along, practically
dragging her faster than her legs could manage
considering her new arrival in the Realms.

"Hurry up!"

"I'm too tired; besides, I think they continued
along the path. There's no sign of them. There's no
need to hurry. We have our entire life."

He stopped only to berate her for her childish
line. "This isn't about 'us' or your concept of what we
are, were, or will become. This is only that I don't
want to see you made a conduit for the soulless ones
to feed off of like some sort of human drip feed."

"But that means that you still love and care for
me."

He started walking again, placing his hand
underneath her elbow to ensure that she kept up with
him. He sighed. "I care for you. I wouldn't want
anything bad to happen to you," he relented.

In spite of his firm grip, Samantha leaned over
and kissed Daniel on the cheek and to her delight, he
didn't stop her. But the moment was broken when the
sound of horses approaching on the embankment
above them.

"Hide!" he said, pulling her behind a cluster of moss-covered boulders. As they continued to traverse the slippery stones, Samantha fell, twisting her ankle and going down hard.

"Just go without me. They won't hurt you."

"I'm not leaving you like this," he said and gallantly scooped her up in his arms.

Samantha wrapped her own arms around his neck and buried her head against his strong shoulders, closing her eyes and relishing the woodsy smell of him that reminded her of their first time together. Too absorbed in her thoughts of Daniel and relishing the plan she had instigated to win him back, she didn't even fear the oncoming horsemen.

# # #

"No sign of her here, Captain," the first horseman shouted just a few feet below where they hid.

"Let's split up and search the area to the east. She was spotted coming this way. We're to bring her back before nightfall when they want to perform the first test. The Circle of Regents intend to be the first to absorb her innocence."

When the horsemen rode past, Daniel helped her to her feet. "Can you stand?"

She tentatively tested her weight on her bad ankle. "I think I can – if you help me," she replied sweetly.

Daniel wrapped his arm around her waist and the one time couple continued on their way back to his cottage.

# # #

Chapter Fifty-Six

"What did they mean when they were talking about my innocence? Because you and I…" Samantha raised her eyebrows in a most non-innocent manner.

"They don't mean that." Unlike Samantha who was relishing the addition of time with Daniel, it was apparent that he didn't want the conversation moving toward more intimate territory. "It refers to your soul. The fact that you've only been motivated by pure thoughts," he explained.

Samantha didn't say a word, but merely smiled trying to evoke the innocence he spoke of. He may have been concerned for her safety, but at that moment she knew there was nothing to fear.

An innocent soul. The very idea of that being used to describe her was ironic. She wondered just how many people perceived her to be one and what they would think if they knew the truth.

Daniel took her silence to be an indication of her nervousness over being found. "Don't worry, Samantha. I won't let anything happen to you."

She took his hand and gave it a light squeeze, knowing just how to play the situation. "I feel so much better and believe me, I don't have any false hope over what your kindness means. I'm just thankful to have you looking out for me. That's all."

Daniel smiled and nodded at her, not even realizing that he was still holding her hand. "That's good. Everything's going to be okay."

"So...about this ritual," she asked. "What happens if they don't find an innocent? Will they keep looking for another?"

"Some people are more innocent than others. Some people's innocence can be completely drained from them. The ritual is performed every time we have a new arrival. It's the government's way of appeasing the people and in truth, they always hope they'll stumble upon a true innocent that will sustain us for years to come. Without the innocents, the people succumb into madness." He shrugged, "The Romani Realms can do that to people."

"But you've been here for years and you're normal."

Again, he chuckled slightly. "Am I?"

"Yes," she said running a hand down the side of his cheek. "You're wonderful...even if you are into someone else," she said quickly, not wanting to rouse suspicion.

They arrived as she spoke and he surveyed his garden, the vegetables planted in neat rows, the fruit trees carefully cultivated. "I work hard to keep things living...to spend time with living creatures. The food I grow sustains me along with the occasional rabbit and bird. It's nice to be around nature rather than swamps."

Samantha laughed. "You think?"

Realizing how crazy the simplicity of the statement could sound to someone who didn't endure the horrors of the Realms everyday, he laughed as well. And when his laughter grew, Samantha joined in and for a moment, it was just as she wanted...the way it used to be.

"Can we go back inside? I'm getting cold." She shivered for good measure and stared up at Daniel with wide eyes.

"Oh sure. I didn't even think about the change in temperature that affects people when they get here. You're probably hungry too."

"A bit," she admitted sweetly.

"Come on." He placed a gentle hand on her back and led her to the house that he had so deliberately tried to have her vacate.

# # #

Darkness was a mere few hours away and Daniel worried about Raven. Not just the fact that he didn't know her whereabouts, but also what he would say when she returned. He paced in front of the window, annoyed that every one of his thoughts veered into two directions regarding her. To tell her about Samantha or hide Samantha away?

He shook his head realizing that was unrealistic since many a night he had to still hide Raven in his basement. He rolled his eyes at the thought of sending both of them down to the basement for a girl's night. As if.

Standing guard in front of the window would give him an edge if he saw any officials from the government approach; he could also use the advanced knowledge of arrival if that person should be Raven. Maybe, just maybe she would be reasonable when seeing another woman in the house...the woman he once loved.

"You okay?" Samantha's voice interrupted his thoughts.

"Yeah, I'm just..." he pointed to the window, the message clear.

"You think they're looking for me already? The officials?"

"I hope not, but I do know that you'll be safe here until they call off the search. Knowing them, that will be nightfall when they give up and feed off one of the more used prisoners. But don't fool yourself into thinking they can sustain off those types. Their mindset is getting warped and they no longer have your wide-eyed outlook about life. That's what they want. It's why they want you."

Samantha stayed quiet, her thoughts churning. "Then why can't you keep me for yourself?"

"It's not right. I realized that after you left...that it was the best thing for everyone involved."

"How can it be right if we both were so upset with the decision?" Her words started to rehash the conversation from earlier.

Daniel clearly seemed to struggle with the memory as he chose his next words carefully. "I'm not sure how long I could keep you innocent. We are pretty sequestered from the world here," he said pointing to his cottage and land.

"But I love being here with you. I don't mind."

"With Raven, it's different," he said bridging the taboo subject. "She has the power and strength that comes from living multiple lives. She doesn't possess innocence so she won't succumb to the madness. It's not a danger for her to be with me."

Daniel said his peace, but his mind remained filled with worry over Raven. She had been gone hours, which wasn't like her. The coup that took over the government and relinquished her power within the council was still in effect. Some residents may have remained indebted to her, but it was a rare one that was willing to stick out their neck in support. Daniel didn't know how long she would have to remain in hiding, but he did know that he was willing to help her for as long as it took.

Turning to Samantha, he decided to reveal what Raven was going through. "Perhaps if you understood some other issues at play, you'll..." his voice trailed. He couldn't rightly say, "you'll just leave" although he hoped the new threat against Samantha would be a passing incident. With renewed hope, he reasoned to himself that Samantha would understand. "There is one thing I didn't tell you about Raven and I..."

Samantha raised an eyebrow, obviously not enjoying the pairing of those two words...Raven and I. "Go on," she said with mild annoyance.

"There are people in charge who have stripped her of authority."

"Really!" Samantha interrupted and leaned forward with more interest than Daniel expected. "How did that happen? When?"

"It's not important. I think it's temporary, but for the time being she's not safe either. However, if push came to shove and they found her…"

"Found her?" Samantha interrupted, picking up on a key phrase.

"Uh, yes. She's not just staying here; she's been sort of hiding out."

Samantha's mouth opened and remained so as if both shocked and pleasured by the new information. Recovering herself, she said, "It's so good of you to come to her rescue."

"Samantha…don't be like that. I explained why we're good for each other and as I was saying, if things got really bad for her I'm prepared to swap my resources for loyalty."

"What do mean? If things got bad?"

"If a resident on the other side discovered that she was here. Although, we're so out of the way I doubt that would ever happen."

Samantha nodded, digesting the information, deciding how to best use the information. "She's mighty lucky to have you." There was an edge to her voice that Daniel picked up on. Immediately, a worrying thought entered his head that he shouldn't have told Samantha so much. But he pushed the thought away, reminding himself that she was a new arrival and as such, she wouldn't be able to hide her innocence. If she harbored ill feelings, she wouldn't be in danger of being captured and used to feed the souls that resided here. There was no way she could cause any harm.

"Don't worry, Samantha. I will keep you safe while there is a threat against you, but I wanted you to know that Raven will be here as well."

"One big happy family," she quipped.

He smiled an uneasy grin, but said nothing.

"Oh Daniel, I'm not being fair," she said noticing his expression. "This can't be easy for you. Let me just say that I understand and I'll do anything to make this situation manageable. I know that Raven can be a bit...jealous." Her voice went down a notch as she emphasized her last word.

"Yeah." There wasn't much else to say and Daniel wasn't sure where she was taking the conversation. That is, until she made her intentions obvious.

"In other words, I don't mind if for the sake of a comfortable living environment, you can relish the use of my innocent mind...even my body."

Samantha swiped off her shirt and stood before Daniel. His eyes took in the sight of her exposed breasts and she noticed the reaction it caused. She stepped forward and stood just inches from him. Moving closer still, she pressed her hips forward so that they lightly touched his. He closed his eyes, struggling with the sensations that were overtaking him. Samantha knew that emotions and sexuality were heightened in the Realms, but there was more to it than that. She also knew that Daniel's reaction meant Raven wasn't the only one who possessed power in this place.

Samantha held a secret. Innocent was not a word that aptly described her. Not in body, nor mind. She had spent months planning for this, aptly manipulating her friends, rehearsing the scenes with

Daniel, and turning over every possibility so that with each direction she controlled the destination.

"Daniel, I know you want to help me because first and foremost, you're a good man." She put her sweater back on in order to make him more comfortable, but she continued her speech. "And second...there's Raven to consider. I came back here for a reason. You will hear me out."

# # #

Chapter Fifty-Seven

The foursome walked across the plains of the Romani Realms on Raven's suggestion. It was a longer route and the openness meant that the sun beat down on them, but unlike the forest that housed many of the soulless residents, it was for the most part a barren stretch of land.

"Are you sure this is wise?" Suki asked as they trudged along.

"It's the best way. Hiding in plain sight," Raven explained. "Trust me...I don't want to be found either."

Suki raised her eyebrows at Raven. "Trust you?"

Raven stopped, placing her hands on her hips. "Okay, gather 'round. We're going to get this hashed out once and for all. And after I'm done talking, you can all decide whether or not to believe that I have no ill intentions toward you. If you don't trust me, go on your way alone and I'll do the same. And certainly, one of our party is likely to get into trouble that way."

"Why is that?" Charlotte asked.

"It's like I said, we're so exposed that the officials wouldn't expect a guilty party to be traveling this way. They want to overthrow my place in the council and are willing to arrest me in order to keep me silent until the new council is in place. They would never expect me to be someplace that makes it so apparently easy to grab me."

James nodded. "She has a point. The same philosophy could be applied to all of us. Each one of us, particularly Charlotte, could be compromised if caught and housed within the Romani Realms for any length of time. People who have something to fear don't put their neck out like this."

"Alrighty...let's keep on this Sunday stroll. It's either the smartest thing we've done or the stupidest," Suki noted and picked up the pace again.

Raven fell into stride next to her. "Isn't that what we said about that double date we had once?" she whispered so the others didn't hear the girl-talk.

"Those twins? Back in London?"

"That was a wild night." Raven smiled at the memory. "You were so funny. I remember you didn't want to kiss the first one until you kissed the second just in case I might get the better twin."

"No. That was your plan," Suki admonished. "You've always been the competitive one."

"Okay, that was me," Raven admitted. "But you said yourself that you wished you had thought of the idea first."

The chatter reminded Suki of the old days with her friend and without thinking she linked her arm in Raven's as they walked. After doing so, Raven stopped for a split second out of surprise, but happy that their relationship was repairing itself after so many years, she carried on without causing a stir.

"Suki?" she said her friend's name as if she had long wanted to hear it fall off her tongue.

"What is it?" The reply was gentle, encouraging.

"I regret so many things. I hope you know that I'm trying to make amends...if it's possible."

Suki nodded, a tear falling from her eye, neither in sadness nor disappointment, but hope. "I know. I've wanted us to be us for just as long. I'm not sure Charlotte will be able to forgive you and because she is my Releasor it does put me in a difficult position."

"She has Phineas and my blessing to be with him. Maybe that can be enough."

Suki looked over her shoulder to where Charlotte and Phineas were trailing behind. She caught Charlotte's eye and raised her eyebrow in question as if to ask if she were alright. Phineas saw the exchange and kissed Charlotte's cheek, a silent statement that told her that he was hers and nothing would come between them.

"I think Charlotte just wants to find her place in this world. She's happy with Phineas, but she's here to find Shadow as well, and of course, to bring back Samantha."

James now caught up and offered his unsolicited opinion. "I couldn't help overhearing you. You know, that's a lofty goal. I know you want to make your Releasors happy, Suki,   but..." He decided not to finish the thought. Like Phineas with Charlotte, or any man with the woman he loves, James just couldn't bear to disappoint Suki.

"I know what James didn't have the heart to say." Raven leaned into Suki and lowered her voice. "It was something short of a miracle that got the five of you out of here last time. Now, you're wanting to add a permanent resident of the Realms to your party...and a minor at that. It's unlikely that Shadow will be able to leave and Suki, if she did..." Raven just shook her head.

James carried on the thought. "Nobody knows what she will be like in the real world. This place changes people."

Suki nodded, hearing their words, however difficult the message.

# # #

Chapter Fifty-Eight

"**D**aniel is going to be worried. I'm never gone this long."

Suki smiled at Raven. "You two...together. I still can't wrap my head around it. I mean, I'm happy for you and you're definitely more capable of surviving here than Samantha. I only hope she's not too disappointed when she learns about your relationship."

Raven got a dreamy look on her face and quickened her step as they approached the cottage. "The last thing I want is to cause any more pain to those girls, but nothing is going to get me to give up my man. I love him, Suki."

Suki squeezed her hand and nodded her understanding. "Samantha was never meant to fall in love here. That was just a strange byproduct of being trapped. I'm happy for you, Raven. Really I am."

"Thanks, Suki. Tomorrow we'll find Samantha and we'll get Daniel to come with us. He can soften the blow and we'll get you all out of here safely."

Suki threw her arms around Raven. "I'll miss you! I never would have thought I'd be doing this." She hugged Raven hard.

"I can't breathe!"

The two were in the throes of laughter as Raven opened the gate leading to the property. "So, are you all wanting dinner or just a snack? Maybe a cup of tea?" Raven offered her fellow travelers. "I even made some scones and strawberry butter with fruit from Daniel's garden."

"You cook?" Suki asked surprised.

"I told you. I've changed. Daniel's been good for me."

They proceeded down the path that twisted around the side of the house and led to the front door that was unusually located in the back garden. They expected it be quiet with the exception of hoping to find Daniel home. What they found, however, were two horses with riders dressed in the official uniform of the Romani Realms council.

"This can't be good," James noted as Raven automatically took a step behind his large frame.

Phineas jumped into action in placing a protective arm around Charlotte to which Raven whispered, "I don't think they're looking for her...or me, for that matter." Stepping into plain view, she explained, "Take a closer look at the horses."

Indeed, the horses nostrils flared as if trying to pick up a scent that was just out of their reach. They turned toward Charlotte, but then back again toward the cottage and whinnied.

The horsemen dismounted and marched to the door. The quartet hurried behind them, shocked at the sight of the first horseman kicking in the door. Samantha and Daniel could be seen sitting on the couch, surprising the group not just with their

presence, but also that their reaction to the intrusion
was totally without worry.

# # #

Chapter Fifty-Nine

S tanding within the doorway, they listened as the horseman read official orders to take Samantha into custody. "...chosen to be the one who will fuel the population with innocent thoughts," they proclaimed along with their final declaration, "She is needed for the greater good."

Raven's confidence was ignited as the horsemen ignored her for Samantha. Speaking up, she bluffed authority, "Who has given this order? I'm on the panel of magistrates and I don't approve it. This party means nothing to you. They are leaving."

The first horseman turned with bored disinterest. "I'm sorry, but you gave up your position when you took up with a human. The government doesn't take kindly to that sort of behavior, but we have decided to look the other way due to the human's sizable donation."

Raven looked at Daniel, trying to read his expression, but he lowered his gaze not meeting her eyes. "Daniel?"

"That donation was more like extortion. I suggest you leave here as I've done everything you've asked. This coming spring will be a bumper crop and you

need my cooperation just as much as I seek solace –
with my friends."

The second horseman drew closer. "Fine. We'll
leave...with her." He moved threateningly close to
Samantha.

"No!" Charlotte called out to which Phineas and
James each instinctively put a hand on her arm.
"Shh," James hissed and Phineas explained, "Don't
bring attention to yourself."

Yet while Charlotte was moved to cry out,
Samantha remained unusually calm, still sitting next
to Daniel. "Darling, we should tell them?" she smiled
at him coquettishly.

"Darling?" Raven picked up on her words
immediately, eyes narrowed at Daniel. "Tell them
what?"

Again, Daniel looked away, pain showing on his
brow. In contrast, Samantha raised her chin and
looked radiant, even victorious.

"Daniel, please answer me." Raven's voice shook
while speaking his name as if deep inside she knew
something was seriously wrong.

His response was to stand and face both
horsemen. Looking them directly in the eye with his
typical calm demeanor, he addressed their request to
leave with Samantha. "You will not be taking
Samantha. As you have already admitted, the
government and I are in good standing. This applies
to my fiancee.

Raven audibly gasped and Samantha smirked at
her response. She never expected Daniel to hurt her
so even if it were obvious that Samantha had
orchestrated it. Suki placed an arm around her

shoulders; the news wasn't good to her ears either. Raven's body shook as silent tears began to flow and she did her best not to release any sound that would betray her pride.

Daniel crossed to her and took her hands in his own. "I'm sorry...please know that I love you."

"Please don't...don't say it. It hurts too much."

Samantha couldn't allow them even those few moments. Rising from her place on the couch, she came to stand next to Daniel, linking her arm through his as she addressed the horsemen. "So you see, there's nothing for any of you here. We're getting married. And that makes me an official, full voting resident of the Romani Realms. I'm one of you now."

Looking toward the group, her voice was gleeful. "I do hope you'll all stay for the wedding." As she locked eyes with Raven, she added, "It's next week."

# # #

Chapter Sixty

"**N**ext week?!" Suki asked with disbelief.

Charlotte, who had remained silently shell-shocked, ran across the room to Samantha. Taking her face in her hands, she forced her friend to look in her eyes as if she couldn't believe that the person announcing this news was her old friend. "Samantha, this is so sudden and from what I've heard, Daniel doesn't feel the same way about you that you do for him. You don't want to enter a loveless marriage. It's not what we always dreamed of as young girls."

Samantha roughly removed Charlotte's hands. "That's just where you're wrong. I'm not that young innocent girl you used to hang out with. The one with a frizzy mane of red hair who the hot boys at school wouldn't give a second glance to. I'm not the one who girls pitied because I was home on the weekends with you. I felt sorry for you so I kept you company. You and your orphaned existence, your boyish awkwardness. But then you changed." Samantha looked at Charlotte with dismay and disgust.

"You became beautiful, Charlotte, and I hated you for it. Boys suddenly wanted you, but you were stuck with me and I knew you'd rather be out."

"That's not true! We're friends!" Charlotte pleaded with Samantha, hoping her anger would turn to reason. "I came all the way here to save you. I risked my life with Phineas for you."

"You see? Talking about a man!"

Phineas shrugged his shoulders and flashed his winning smile. "Don't blame the entire species. You've got one sitting right there on the couch." He nodded to Daniel. "Sorry bro, I don't mean to get you into a tighter spot than you already are."

Samantha jumped back into the conversation. "Tighter spot? Is that what you think? He loved me once and he'll do so again."

Raven found her old bravado. "Really? I never threw myself at a man. Nor manipulated my way into someone's arms. James. Phineas. Daniel. Not one of them was with me out of some sick coercion. Circumstance maybe. But real feelings developed. And then, when time moved forward and sometimes feelings shift, I moved on like a real woman. I held my head up high and I accepted that they also moved on. But that is not what has happened between you and Daniel."

Raven looked to Daniel once more and this time, to Samantha's chagrin, he held her gaze and what passed between them was captured and seen by everyone in the room. Love. And sadly, love that was being stripped away from them.

"Shut up!" Samantha's anger exploded. "Raven, you have held power for centuries and then it was stripped away from you. You should thank me. Your power here is restored. Your place on the council is back. All they wanted was reassurance of a human drip feed and I'm happy to give them that."

Suki shook her head, not wanting to hear it. "How can you do this?"

"Because Suki, don't you understand?" Samantha turned to look at Charlotte before answering and then, seeing her friend's bewildered expression, she laughed heartily. "You two never understood. I'm not an innocent. I never have been. Charlotte, you and I were never alike. You're so prim and proper. Cool and collected. I never saw a bit of fire within you...that is, not until the idea of Shadow came along."

Charlotte swallowed hard, afraid of asking the question that so desperately wanted to fall off her tongue. "What do you mean... "the idea" of Shadow?"

Samantha raised her hands above her head in a 'hallelujah' movement. Her thoughts further igniting hurtful emotions that she couldn't wait to free. "I learned early on when I first came here that we see what we want to see. When you arrived, it was so easy to plant the seed for the child you so desperately wanted. The child that you can nourish and look after in the way that you never received. Shadow is my creation. Yes, she was meant for you, but not in the way that you think."

"No!" Charlotte threw herself at Phineas. "It's not true. Tell me it's not. You saw her. You know she's meant to be ours."

"Mmm, not so much," Samantha answered coldly. "But she was a surefire way to get you back here. Guess you'll just have to wait for a baby like the rest of us. Ooh, that is if you ever get that wedding you wanted."

Samantha ignored Charlotte's horrified expression and simply crossed the room to Daniel, placing a hand on his shoulder. "Personally, I think you should thank me, Charlotte. Imagine all the fun you and Phineas will have trying to make a child. I know that Daniel and I look forward to doing just that." With the last statement, she flashed a mean-spirited, toothy grin in Raven's direction to which the cast off beauty placed a comforting hand on Charlotte's back as she wept in Phineas' arms.

"Charlotte, please don't cry," Phineas kissed the top of her head. "You never saw what I did in Shadow because you so desperately wanted her to be ours. But she never was what you believed her to be. Come on," he picked up her chin, looking her in the eyes. "We fought about this back home and now we know the reason. Nothing is going to break us apart...certainly not a child born out of our love. When the time is right, we will have a baby."

Charlotte nodded her head and wiped away her tears. Phineas' words were true and they resonated with her. "I love you," she whispered.

Phineas kissed her lips, softly and with promise of a future together.

But the gesture was interrupted by gagging noises from Samantha. "Gross."

Charlotte narrowed her eyes. "What's happened to you? Is this really what you want? One last chance, Samantha. Say it right now...say that you want to go back and be the way we used to be and all is forgiven. Just come back to us. Let us see that beautiful, innocent girl that we know."

"Innocence?" she laughed, releasing a hearty and phony chuckle. "It's not there. And don't think the Romani Realms took it from me. I want to be here. What they're getting is a human that is immune to atrocities and to them, that is very interesting and highly appealing. They live for it. Unlike innocence, which can vanish or be used up, apathy sustains. And I don't give a damn."

The room was silent until Samantha delivered the final blow.

"The gazebo was booked all this week or I would have hurried the ceremony along. I hope you all won't be uncomfortable waiting a week. I would put you up in our place, but somehow I think it would just feel a bit...crowded." Her voice took on a sweet tone, but she was clearly a changed person.

"Stop. Just stop for a minute." Daniel admonished and then speaking more to Raven than anyone he announced, "Please know that there wasn't a choice. It was the only way for..."

"That's enough, sweetie," Samantha interrupted. "I want to get with Suki and Charlotte and talk bridesmaid dresses."

Suki nodded her head sadly. Charlotte just stared, a vacant expression crossing her features as she clearly did not recognize her friend.

"Oh, come on now. Why do you all look so serious? A wedding is a happy occasion. I know that you're probably worried about me deciding to live so far away from home, but there won't be any threats to me here anymore. Not with Daniel...so, don't you see? I've gotten what we set out to do. This is what we all wanted, isn't it?"

"It's only what you wanted," Raven spoke, a lone voice in the hushed crowd.

"Come on, Raven," Samantha chided. "It was our raison d'etre! Our reason to be...the sole purpose of our little outing to this charming locale of yours."

"Samantha, that's enough!" Daniel hissed and pulled her arm, leading her away from the others. "I will marry you because it's the only way to keep Raven from harm. One life for the other. As you said, you're nothing but a drip feed to this society. Less you forget that my deal with the government extended beyond just providing a few strawberries to them in exchange for your safety. It's safe passage for all of them and a guarantee that my farm will not be taken away. You put all of us in jeopardy by parading yourself here. Don't you ever forget what I have sacrificed."

Having said his peace, Daniel returned to the group with Samantha on his heels. Flashing a vibrant smile, Samantha carried on with her new role as bride-to-be. "I'm planning a small tea later this afternoon for all out of town guests. So, I'll see you back here at three o'clock. So sorry for the late notice. I wish there was more time before my wedding."

James and Phineas stood awkwardly with their hands in their pockets, looking to Charlotte and Suki for an appropriate reaction. But the girls seemed unable to verbalize a proper response either, just looking to each other in a helpless exchange of non-verbal communication. It was only Raven that had the fortitude to speak what was on everyone's mind.

"Samantha!" she called out as the red-headed girl turned her back to them, heading toward her bedroom – the one that Raven had believed was her own, just a day earlier.

"Oh yes, Raven? Did you have something to add?" Samantha asked with false sweetness.

"Don't wish for anything on my account. Ever. If wishes were horses, beggars would ride."

# # #

"Where to?" Charlotte asked Phineas, who in turn gave a questioning glance to Suki and James. "It's not like there's a Starbucks where we can hang."

In contrast to the two couples who stood huddled together at the edge of the path leading back toward the meadow and main amphitheater and square, Raven sat on the small wooden bench that overlooked Daniel's property. Staring at the fields that she had tended with him, her expression was wistful. Phineas glanced over at her expecting to recognize the mood that typically led Raven to hatch a plot of revenge, but there was nothing. Just resolve.

"Give me a minute," he said to Charlotte, motioning to Raven. "I need to be the one to talk to her."

Charlotte glanced over, hesitated briefly, but nodded. There was no threat to her from Raven either physically or emotionally. Phineas was her man now, but she recognized as he did, the years...centuries he had spent with Raven and she needed her former confidante. "Go on. Maybe you can pull her out of the doldrums."

For a moment Phineas didn't say a word. He just sat down next to Raven. Sometimes, having someone near is enough. No words were spoken. The warmth he exuded and sent to Raven seemed to thaw the emotions that she held in tight control.

One tear fell from her eye and once it was loose, others quickly followed. He let her weep and mourn for as long as she needed knowing that his presence was the support she needed. Wiping away her tears, she finally spoke. "I thought I could just stay numb. Accept it."

"No. That's resolve and it's the last emotion that people feel when they're trapped here. You can't become that type of a person – just a shell of your former self. That's not the Raven I know and still love."

She turned to him, and a smile crossed her face unlike any he had seen in his past with her. It had a purity to it. It was genuine with appreciation. "You mean that, don't you? You will always be my friend as well, Phin. And I'm so thankful to have Suki back."

"Maybe that's the good that has come out of this." He took her hand and gave it a light squeeze.

"I think so. I have to believe in something good." She stood up as if to say she was ready to leave. "But..."

"But?" he arched an eyebrow at her. "Something in your tone tells me that I'm hearing a bit of the old Raven coming through."

"Well, maybe my old self, combined with a wiser, new self. I'm going to need everyone's help."

# # #

Chapter Sixty-One

Phineas walked Raven over to the group, specifically Charlotte. The two women stared at each other without speaking as there was just too much to say for one to know where to begin.

With Phineas standing shoulder to shoulder with Raven, Charlotte decided it was her job to break the ice if for no other reason than to get her man back by her side. "I forgive you," she said simply to Raven.

Raven nodded and then added her own sentiment. "I made mistakes. Maybe I had reason to be hurt, but that doesn't excuse what happened last year"

"You've changed," Charlotte admitted and then, thinking of Samantha, she added with a sad note, "people change."

Raven nodded and although physical contact was difficult for her, she patted Charlotte's arm a couple times, more like one would do to a dog you're not sure is friendly, before stepping back again. Charlotte took the gesture as an opportunity to ask Raven the question that was on everyone's mind. "Is Samantha lost to this place? Did the Romani Realms do this to her or was she always..."

"Evil?" Raven filled in the blank.

Charlotte looked pained, but nodded.

"The Romani Realms only accentuates one's emotions and brings out what is already within. I'd say this is the real Samantha." Raven turned to Suki, both to ensure she wasn't hurt by the accusation against one of her Releasors and to confirm her suspicions.

"She was always fiery...impetuous. I just thought it was something she would outgrow, but instead it was something that continued to grow from within. From the first day when I was still trapped within my bottle, I heard the desire in her voice. At the time, she was trying to wrangle a school girl crush. You remember that, Charlotte?"

"Ryan and Josh...Samantha had a plan for stealing them away from their girlfriends. I remember she was on a mission. It's funny how I thought there was something wrong with me for hanging in the background. I never pursued things the way she did."

Suki gave her a brief hug. "There's nothing wrong with you. Never has been. The way I was raised in the South meant that being reserved was to be a lady. Not that Samantha didn't possess admirable qualities, but to analyze them now, I can see that her 'can-do' attitude was more akin to 'take no prisoners.' I think she always wanted to change you, Charlotte, and that's not what a friend does."

Suki remained thoughtful, her mind returning to the time of her release. "You had nothing that needed to change. Samantha made you take a hard look at yourself in the mirror – your clothes, your posture –

and she said that you two were average. That wasn't true then and it's not true now. I'm sorry for my part in giving you a makeover when I appeared."

Charlotte laughed. "That was fun! Who doesn't like a spa day? Suki, you never made me feel as if I weren't good enough. Samantha was the one who always had a plan to change the way we lived. Looking back now, I wonder if that's why she made a play for your bottle."

"It was supposed to be you, Charlotte. You were the one to originally find my bottle...to hold it. But your kindness...you immediately shared it with Samantha when she set her sights on it."

Charlotte hunched up her shoulders. "I can't take it back now."

"No, but you can learn from it," Raven piped up. "Charlotte...Suki...I have an idea. I think you two can use the past to make a difference in the future."

Suki looked to Charlotte and then back again at Raven, trying to decide if the idea that just launched in her mind grew there organically or was placed by Raven. "I think I know what you're thinking, but I can't be the one..."

Without missing a beat, Charlotte finished her thought showing that she knew exactly what the other two women were thinking. "But I can! I'm your Releasor and there's one last wish. I can use it."

Raven and Suki sent Charlotte smiles of pride. "By George I think she's got it." Raven quipped to which Suki responded, "You shan't be a Sowce, the better for what's in it."

"Okay, girls...you've lost me somewhere around the 1600s. Can we come back to modern day?"

Raven and Suki put their arms around each other's shoulders and huddled closely with Charlotte, the three of them putting their heads together. "There's only one way," Suki began.

# # #

Chapter Sixty-Two

T he bride looked radiant and the groom appeared so nervous that it was no wonder the doors were guarded by military officials. Had that bride been anyone other than Samantha and had she not virtually highjacked Daniel, there may have been cause for celebration. But as it stood, the guests meandered amidst the high standing tables that displayed offerings of canapes and cocktails whispering gossip predictions about the marital end before its beginning.

Samantha sought out Suki and Charlotte as they worked their way through their second cocktails. "Hey, go easy on those. I need my bridesmaids to be at their best."

Charlotte, who normally refrained from drinking, was making up for lost time. She responded by raising her glass to Samantha and taking a healthy swig. "To weddings!" she slurred. "It may not be mine, but the wine is fine."

"Can't you do something about her?" Samantha barked at Suki. "Honestly, as a genie to us you are something of a disappointment. I've had to make so

many of my dreams come true on my own. This
wedding is testament to that."

Suki looked at her demurely. "I merely serve your
wishes."

"Whatever. Come on, you two...procession...now.
Let's get our wedding on."

# # #

Phineas and James made handsome groomsmen as
they waited at the end of the aisle with Daniel inside
the grand amphitheater. James and Phineas wore
black tuxedos with white shirts and white rose
boutineers. Daniel was dressed in the same stylish
black and white, but wore a red rose as insisted by
Samantha who wanted the traditional symbol of love
to be scattered throughout the room.

In addition to the red roses, a bevy of red-winged
butterflies darted about the room. Rather than seem
peaceful, the insects dive-bombed the guests and
fluttered against the windows as if even they wanted
to leave the spectacle. The room was further
decorated in opulent gold to match Samantha's
unconventional wedding gown of the same color.
Raven knew that she and Daniel had been intimate,
but Samantha's declaration that a white wedding
dress would not be appropriate still hurt her wounded
heart.

Even worse, the wedding was declared an official
government event and since she had been reinstated
with all charges of treason dropped, it was insisted
that she attend the wedding in an official capacity.
She sat on the groom's side of the aisle as that seemed

more appropriate to her and at least she reasoned that her presence there could offer some support to Daniel, whose eye caught hers more frequently than was proper.

"Don't do it, man," Phineas leaned into Daniel's ear. "Samantha seems likely to go ballistic if she catches you making eyes at Raven and something tells me you've got more than a few years to spend with her."

Daniel exhaled deeply, not wanting to be reminded of how slowly time can pass in the Realms. "At least I didn't have to plan this monstrosity of an event. Samantha spent all her time doing it. The only saving grace was that the council insisted we sleep in separate homes during the wedding planning stage. Something about wanting to instill hope and tradition back to the Romani Realms."

James added his thoughts on the subject, "Maybe they're going for a kinder, gentler Realms where people don't feed on each other's minds until after the honeymoon."

"I feel better, James. Thanks."

James smiled at Daniel and gave him a friendly punch in the arm. "Any time. It's all about perspective."

The music started and as it did, the doors at the back of the theater opened revealing Suki standing there in an elegant black dress carrying a small nosegay of red roses. As she started to walk, Charlotte proceeded into the room behind her. With her white blonde hair, she looked equally stunning, perhaps more so in the contrasting black gown.

"Whoa..." Phineas breathed softly. "I wish I could take your place."

"Me too," Daniel muttered.

The women reached the end of the aisle and took their places. The judge of the Romani Realms approached and stood behind a podium, then signaled the organist to play. The four familiar notes of the wedding procession started and Samantha glided down the aisle, beaming at Daniel all the way.

When she reached her destination next to Daniel the usual niceties were spoken by the judge – a poem about love everlasting, a Bible verse about the birth of time and man and woman's place in our world. Surprisingly, a majority of the congregation murmured their approval after the verse was spoken as if the Romani Realms was the modern equivalent for the Garden of Eden and Daniel and Samantha were their Adam and Eve. Only the foursome that stood alongside the bride and groom looked displeased.

In fact, it wasn't just displeasure that crossed the features of Suki and Charlotte. It was anxiousness, a nervous time bomb of expectation and waiting. Each one wondering when the time would come that they could object to this union.

The moment arrived and Suki didn't hesitate. "I have something to say...information that will make it impossible for this union to occur."

A hush fell over the congregation, but the judge laid his black and angry eyes on Suki. He was a surly man who didn't take kindly to having his time as the center of attention stolen away. He bristled and made it known that this was most unconventional. "What do you have to say for yourself?"

"I am Samantha's genie, obligated to deliver three wishes of which two have been used. The third was made last week and I intend to uphold the letter of the law."

"State this wish," the judge ordered.

"She said, and I quote, 'I wish there was more time before my wedding.' My intention is to give Samantha her wish...with indefinite time before her wedding."

"It's ambiguous. I don't recognize this as a valid reason to stop this wedding."

The crowd began to clap a civilized thunder of approval.

"It's not for you to say." Suki stood a bit taller, allowing her voice to ring strong.

"Are you saying that the period of time before her wedding will repeat until infinity?"

Making sure that there could be no misunderstanding, Suki spoke her next words with careful clarity. "She wished for more time before the wedding. I will provide that to her. She will have all the time in the world."

"No!" Samantha spoke for the first time since the exchange began, now fully understanding what Suki had in mind and fearful of the possibility. "I am what the Romani Realms has always wanted. Grant my wedding and I will serve you with my own soul without your people ever having to worry about lost innocence."

"You can't overstep my boundaries," Suki spoke before any decisions could be made. "The laws of genies go back thousands of years."

The judge looked from Suki to Samantha; he raised his hands as if in apology to both. "This is meant to be a happy occasion. I understand your commitment and responsibility to the bride," he said to Suki, "but, I cannot turn the Romani Realms into a purgatory where each day is the same as the last, constantly waiting for a wedding that will never be. Our people wouldn't want to think of our Realms in that light."

Suki shook her head sadly. Eyeing Charlotte, her glance spoke volumes, showing her regret. Speaking softly, she made one last attempt, knowing the answer before asking her question. "What becomes of my responsibility?"

The judge looked to Samantha, who nodded approval. "Tell her," she ordered.

"You are released of your duties. You are not beholden to Samantha any longer."

A single tear weaved its way down Suki's face as the reality of her loss set in. She once loved Samantha like a mother with hopes for her future and dreams for her happiness. This wasn't the ending of their relationship that she had envisioned. Charlotte took her hand and gave it a squeeze of reassurance.

James snuck his arm around her back, but remained standing at attention looking the perfect part of a groomsman while still supporting his love. He winked at her, an indication to Suki that she still had someone who supported her by her side.

Taking a deep breath, she nodded once to the judge indicating that if he must proceed then he may.

"If there are no further concerns, we will continue with this most beautiful ceremony."

The words from the judge passed in a dizzy haze as the wedding party stood by Samantha's side dutifully and without further interruption. But one subtle movement from the congregation caught only Raven's eye. It wasn't enough of a distraction to be considered a disturbance, but it was a distinct attempt to get Samantha's attention that fulfilled its every intention. Raven removed her scarf. Such a simple action, but one with a myriad of ramifications.

There, resting on Raven's collarbone sat a beautiful necklace – a deep blue stone the color of Suki's bottle...the Amulet of Pollox. This powerful pendant had been carefully guarded by Suki for centuries until Charlotte took possession of it. It held the knowledge from every great man that Suki ever served and with Charlotte's didactic memory, that knowledge was hers. When they were earlier at odds with Raven, they kept the necklace from her, unsure of what she would do with the knowledge accumulated from it.

But in a show of solidarity and renewed trust, Charlotte and Suki endowed the necklace to Raven. After all, both of the women still obtained the knowledge it possessed. Their only reason to keep it within their possession was simply to keep it away from the wrong hands.

Their decision to give it to Raven was not made without long hours of thought and because Raven never asked for the gift, Suki and Charlotte were assured that their decision was both right and just. Raven had centuries of knowledge, enough wisdom of humanity's goodness and evil, both of which were important lessons for those living in the Romani Realms. But more importantly, they gave the necklace to Raven as a form of insurance – in case Suki's plan to grant Samantha's third wish was not accepted.

Suki also wanted Raven to have the pendant in order to keep her safe within the Romani Realms should another government uprising ever occur. The pendant would give her bargaining power. It would also serve as a conduit directly to Suki should Raven ever need her. And, it would be a constant reminder to Samantha that she couldn't manipulate every situation to her desires.

Samantha stared at Raven a beat too long as the judge repeated his question of whether she took this man standing before the congregation as her lawful husband.

She shook herself out of her reverie and turned her attention to Daniel, smiling with the knowledge that there was one thing Raven didn't get. "Yes, I do!" she answered.

"And do you, Daniel?" the judge droned on with the same question to which Daniel also responded in the affirmative although with visibly less enthusiasm.

# # #

Epilogue

The party-goers stood in a line waiting to congratulate the newly married couple. Among them was Raven, whose stoic expression was easy to wear. She needn't make pleasant conversation with anyone for she now refused to view her fellow magistrates on the council as comrades. If they tried to overthrow her once, they could certainly do so again. The only difference was that now it would be impossible for them to do so, although she was sure that plenty would still wish they could try. Raven viewed the Romani Realms in the same manner as the real world – ever-changing and not necessarily for the good.

Throughout history politicians came into power to please some and disappoint others. Dictators would rise and fall as did entire civilizations. Celebrities would come into favor and then fall from grace. Raven contemplated her place in this world as couples circled the dance floor.

There was a time when she hated Samantha and Charlotte for what they represented. Two teenage girls who had the accidental good fortune to stumble upon a genie's bottle. It launched them into a world of privilege where any three wishes could be granted along with a pendant that would reveal great secrets. Unlike their random discovery, Raven had spent centuries learning skills, meeting people, and surviving. She never relied on anyone...until recently.

The jealousy and ambition that had driven her to seek revenge were tamed through love...and perhaps her own misfortune. It had taken her losing power after living with extreme control to see what was important in the world. Secrets and skills, power and control had nothing over a life of simple happiness with a man whom she loved and friends whom she cared for.

She sighed, letting her shoulders rise and fall. She lost the man, although in her heart she knew that Daniel was still hers. Samantha may have outplayed her where he was concerned, but she could take solace in the fact that she could come and go from the Romani Realms as she pleased and by her side would be Suki. She had even gained a new friend in Charlotte and with the forgiveness that she showed Charlotte, her relationship with Phineas was restored and along with him, a friendship with James as well.

"Four friends gained, one love lost. I suppose I'm ahead of the game," she muttered to herself while watching Samantha and Daniel twirl in the center of the dance floor.

"Did you say something Miss Raven?"

Two council guards stood nearby, each one flanking Raven as she leaned against the wall listening to the methodical waltz that was heard from a non-existent orchestra, playing a tinny sound that seemed to come from everywhere. Raven shook her head while watching the couples twirl like ice skaters rotating on a music box.

The guard to her left commented, "I hear you live for another day."

"So it would appear," she answered without emotion.

"For what it's worth, I always liked your ideas...when you were part of the magistrates."

"Good to know. Maybe I'll come back on board. There doesn't seem to be much else for me here."

Both guards looked out to the dance floor following Raven's gaze to where Daniel and Samantha danced.

Raven moved to a nearby table and the two guards followed, each taking a seat next to her. The three sat for another moment in silence. Raven crosses her legs, revealing thigh high black boots that stopped just south of a patch of creamy white skin that was graced by a lacy, suspender belt.

The first guard addresses the second, speaking over Raven as if she weren't there. "She's just too damned pretty."

"Don't," the second guard says. "Don't go there."

"What are you two oafs babbling about? I'm right here."

The first guard leaned closer, whispering in her ear. "You should leave. Go to your home now."

"Home? And where would that be? Up until last week I was living at Daniel's because your comrades decided to completely make a mess of my place. So you'll understand if I'm not super anxious to go back to my hovel."

He reached gently for her elbow, trying to pull her up to a standing position. "Go back. I'll help you clean it up...after."

"After? After what?"

"George, shut up! You've said enough," the second guard barked.

"You want to leave her here after she ruled us for two years? You pledged allegiance to her once. Terence, if we save her, we have a chance at saving our own humanity."

"Whatever you're trying to do, it won't work." Raven spoke, the sorrow clear in her tone. "There is no humanity here. This place robs every single person of it."

Her sentiment was enough to inspire both guards to prove her wrong. They looked to each other and nodded a signal before each grabbed one of Raven's arms, pulling her up from her chair and leading her toward the exit.

"Fine...why should I stay where I'm not wanted?"

"You are wanted. That's why you have to leave. You only have a minute, maybe two."

Raven sensed the true urgency. She eyed both men and then let her eyes dart about the room. Not seeing anything out of the ordinary, she addressed them once more. "What's about to happen?"

"Just go! Now!" The men led her to the exit and then returned quickly to the direction they had left, pulling out gas masks from the backpacks they had stashed by the exit. Raven watched the scene unfold from just outside the amphitheater doors, remaining a far enough distance away to stay safe from the sudden explosion that rocked the building.

Shards of glass from the surrounding windows shattered and flew throughout the space cutting dancers who still remained on the floor. Those who weren't accosted by the glass couldn't escape the rain of debris that fell from the ceiling. The space filled with dust as well as a sickly sweet smell emitted from the bombs that the guards had diffused.

Raven watched on in horror from her vantage point as people screamed and tried to run to safety, but the doors had been closed and locked. She pushed against the one door that she had been led through to no avail. Searching for an alternate entrance, she finally noticed a small ventilation duct at the ground level of the main ballroom. The metal grates were blocked, but she managed to kick at the bars until it gave away. Pulling herself through, she made her way into the melee.

Curtains that covered the windows had now caught fire. Within minutes the flames would mix with the noxious gas and everyone would be in grave jeopardy.

Her long time connection to Phineas led her to him immediately. "Phineas!" she shouted to her former lover and protege. "Here!"

With relief, she saw that he had seen the slight opening and pulled himself and Charlotte through it.

She spotted Suki with James and was relieved that both were already making their way toward her. "Raven, the exits are blocked," Suki shouted.

"There! There's an opening," Raven pointed and raised her voice above the screaming crowd.

Suki turned to where she pointed, but no sooner turned back when she saw Raven returning to the ballroom. "Raven!"

"No, Suki. You go."

"Please Raven. Being with you again is the cat's pajamas. I'm not leaving without you."

"I have to help Daniel."

"You can't save him from this place," Suki said sadly, relishing every moment with Raven as she suspected that it may once again be her last.

Raven simply shook her head and walked to the center of the room, putting herself directly in the line of the guard's fire as they had now started to rid the room of anyone who survived the bombing with their own might.

She took one shot in the shoulder, but kept going as Daniel was in her sights. As bodies fell around her she maintained her pace. Another blast shook the room and a section of the ceiling crashed onto her, causing her to lose her footing. But Raven was determined and only remained down for a few moments. She crawled to breathe in cleaner air and once near Daniel, she reached up to him and nearly cried for all she had lost when he took her hand.

Their eyes showed the love between them, but there was no time for sentiment. Placing a weak hand on his shoulder, she gave him a weary smile. "You need to leave...with her." Raven jutted her chin toward the hidden opening. "The others made it out. It's your turn."

"They won't hurt us," Daniel declared. "She's made a deal with the government. She's practically Romani Realms royalty now."

"You can't rely on her promises to feed the soulless ones. Eventually, any innocence within her will be drained. It's why they bombed the place," she said knowingly. "They'll drain the bodies and store their innocence for when it's needed.'

"They'll have plenty to go around," Daniel said sadly. "Samantha has seen to that. She's promised them her firstborn."

Raven opened her arms to Daniel as he practically crumpled, his head resting on her shoulder. "I'm so sorry, Daniel."

"I love you, Raven."

She sobbed. For the first time since Samantha came between them, she let the tears fall fast. It felt good to lose control if it meant letting Daniel see how she felt toward him.

"You can't trust them...any of them." She said the last thought even before Samantha approached, but it was clear to Daniel whom she referred to. It made Raven's next move even more surprising. As one of the guards raised his weapon and pointed at Samantha, Raven jumped in the line of the bullet.

"Why? Why would you do this?" Samantha looked down at her. "It's so like you to try anything to get his attention."

"Samantha!" Daniel spat her name with disgust as he ran to Raven, cradling her head in his lap. "Guards! Please somebody help her."

The guards who had once been forced to turn their backs on Raven now universally came to attention. Orders were called into walkie-talkies that the bombing had been a success with the exception of one mistaken casualty.

"Help is on its way," a guard reported to Daniel. "Here," he tossed him a towel to aid him in stopping the bleeding. "Tell her to hold on."

"That won't do her any good. Just look at that nasty wound she's earned herself." Samantha cast the nasty sentiment as she stared at Daniel and Raven huddled together.

Blood spilled from Raven's chest, making her breathing shallow, but she still managed to get the last of her words out. "I know when I'm not wanted. I have pride."

"That hasn't stopped you in the past," Samantha said like a spoiled child.

"Enough Samantha! You've done enough," Daniel spoke sternly at his new bride while smoothing back Raven's hair and bending his head down to hers. He held her as close as he could without hurting her. "Don't speak," he urged.

But Raven had remained silent during a very painful ceremony and if this were her last breaths she would say her peace.

"The past was different. I used to wish for your unhappiness...all of you, who seemed to get everything on a silver platter. That's not what I want now."

Samantha sneered at her. "Well...what is it, then? What do you want?"

"Redemption."

# # #

The Romani Realms

Released

Resurrected

Returned

"Redemption" - Coming 2016

Books by Mia Fox

Romani Realms Series

Released (book 1)
Resurrected (book 2)
Returned (book 3)

Chasing Shadows Series

Believe (book 1)
Trust (book 2)

Hollywood Hotties Series

Alert the Media (stand alone book)
Keeping Up (stand alone book)

Guardian Angel Series

Malibu Angel (book 1)

Surprise Passion Series

Ready for the Yeti (book 1)
Going Steady with the Yeti (book 2)
Ethel and the Merman (book 3)
Scent of the Centaur (book 4)

About the Author

Mia Fox is a Los Angeles-based novelist who writes across varied genres including Young Adult/New Adult Paranormal Romance and Chick Lit. She received her Bachelor of Arts Degree in Communications from U.S.C. followed by a Masters Degree in Professional Writing also from U.S.C.

A lifelong reader and history lover, Mia loves infusing her own writing with details of the past. Her other interests include cooking and baking. Fortunately, she is also a yoga enthusiast, which proves useful in keeping her other passion – eating – in check.

Mia is happily married to her best-friend, a Brit who has inspired her with annual visits to England, an appreciation for dark chocolate, and the blessing of their three children.

Mia's books are available from Amazon, Barnes and Noble, iBooks, and Kobo.

Stay in touch with Mia Fox

Website
http://miafox.net/

Amazon
http://www.amazon.com/Mia-Fox/e/B00CXZQ84C

Facebook
https://www.facebook.com/MiaFoxBooks

Twitter
https://twitter.com/MiaFoxBooks

Goodreads
https://www.goodreads.com/author/show/7036109.
Mia_Fox

Pinterest
https://www.pinterest.com/miafoxbooks/

Instagram
https://instagram.com/MiaFoxBooks

Booktropolous Social
https://booktropoloussocial.com/index.php?do=/pro
file-2507/

Tumblr
http://miafoxbooks.tumblr.com/

Tsu
http://www.tsu.co/MiaFoxBooks